# World-Mart

# WORLD-MART

Leigh M. Lane

Cerebral Books
Henderson, NV

Second Edition Printing

23 22 21 20 19 18 17 16 15          1 2 3 4 5 6 7 8 9 10

ISBN: 1518744435
ISBN-13: 978-1518744433

For Diana.

# Chapter One

George Irwin sat at his desk, shuffling through pages of paperwork, cross-referencing the various pieces of information his research associates had previously uncovered and filed. His tiny cubicle was identical to the hundreds of other cubicles strategically placed throughout the large, cold room, but subtly personalized with a framed picture of his wife and two kids. He drank tepid water from a coffee cup that boasted "#1 Dad" along each side. Both were Corporate-issued, varying from those of George's neighbors only by the pictures they contained and the "#1" slogan listed on their cups.

The building had no windows, as Law-Corp's top managers had determined that windows only wasted resources and allowed for distraction. George was a research manager, which entailed collecting, checking, and re-filing all of the paperwork filed by his research associates. Despite being born to two Mart parents, and mainly due to his score of 550 on the Corporate Intelligence Quantifier Test, George had been fortunate enough to have been placed in the

Corp Segregate. Although he could never aspire for anything higher than lower management, George had risen higher in status than most simple Mart employees could ever hope for. He was able to provide for his family in ways his parents never could have, and that alone was enough to keep him complacent despite the stress and monotony. George was proud to be a research manager for Law-Corp #01025, and he worked hard to ensure his job security at the firm.

Despite being in his early forties, George was in good shape and still held a youthful appearance. He and his wife, a smart and lovely woman who also worked in the Corp Segregate, had married young. A few years George's junior, Virginia worked as a call center associate for Communications-Corp #12668. They had two children: fifteen-year-old Shelley and seven-year-old Kurt, both of whom were enrolled in the Corp Education System. Much of George and Virginia's income went toward keeping their children in the system, but their superior education would ensure lower to middle management Corp jobs for both of them.

George glanced through the electronic file of a doctor charged with prescribing and selling antibiotics. The research associates who put the case together had been thorough. The evidence against the doctor was overwhelming, and one particular patient the doctor attempted to treat had been infected with strep throat. Of course, when top managers confirmed that the patient was indeed ill with strep, Police-Corp and Medical-Corp worked together to euthanize the man as quickly and humanely as possible.

Antibiotics had been outlawed nearly twenty years ago, after scientists had determined their use was no longer effective against most life-threatening disease-causing bacteria. Even worse, antibiotics affected certain bacteria's evolutionary development, causing even some of the most benign of infections eventually to become untreatable and deadly. Antibiotic-immune strep, staph, and tuberculosis had become epidemic before George was born, but he'd heard the stories about how quickly the three had threatened the entire human population and how Medical-Corp had finally intervened. Its top managers ordered the construction of quarantine camps, where hundreds of thousands of people eventually were corralled, killed, and cremated. All suspected cases of serious infectious diseases were now referred to a special committee within Medical-Corp. All whom they deemed infectious were removed for the greater good of society.

George looked through the different studies attached to the case. Everything looked straightforward, except for the defendant's personal notes. Page after page, almost all of the doctor's words were blacked out, all pertaining to an apparent case study he'd been conducting. The only reason the research associate had left in the scanned files was that every few pages had untouched text in which the doctor mentioned his prescribing illegal antibiotics. George agreed to keep the otherwise useless pages in the file, deciding that the prosecution managers would likely find some use for them.

He read the pages of receipts, recorded telephone conversations, and photocopies of the doctor's appointment logs. Everything appeared to be in order. Police-Corp already had a confession from the man, and therefore a guilty verdict from Law-Corp's high management was already imminent. Still, it was George's job to suggest formally that the doctor be charged and his file be sent to Sentencing. He entered the computer database in front of him, scanning the doctor's charge sheet and bringing it to the monitor.

Two virtual buttons bearing the words "Guilty" and "Not Guilty" appeared on the bottom right corner of the screen under the word "Recommendation." George tapped the "Guilty" button, prompting a new screen to appear with a series of questions for which George had the option to agree or disagree with his associates' previous responses:

Did the Defendant confess to his/her crime(s)?
(Research associate #00335-921 said "Yes.")
Click HERE to agree.
Click HERE to disagree.

Does the file work indicate that the Defendant showed remorse for said crime(s)?
(Research associate #01002-486 said "No.")
Click HERE to agree.
Click HERE to disagree.

Does the file work indicate that the Defendant could have made a profit by committing said crime(s)?
(Research associate #00335-921 said "Yes.")
Click HERE to agree.
Click HERE to disagree.

Has the Defendant ever been convicted of any previous crimes?

(Research associate #00257-851 said "Yes.")

Click HERE to agree.

Click HERE to disagree.

Does the Defendant have anything to say in his/her defense, for having committed said crime(s)?

(Research associate #01014-002 said "Yes.")

Click HERE to agree.

Click HERE to disagree.

George used another application to search for his answers. He went through each relevant section of file work, double-checking himself before punching in the same answers as given by the other research associates.

The computer then prompted, "State Defendant's argument (limit 140 characters)," and George navigated through the file. He found the transcripts from the doctor's police interview. He frowned as he found the lines in which the doctor said he could explain himself, but the explanation was blacked out. He studied the few words that remained between the thick swatches of black ink, trying to see if even a gist of the man's argument remained. Knowing that files were blacked out when a suspect's text referred to useless or misleading concepts, he knew nothing else could be done but type, "Defendant's argument invalid."

The computer asked him if he was sure, and George tapped a round button with a "Yes" stretched across it.

The printer spat out a few sheets of new paperwork. It was an old, loud, outdated machine, and the paper it used was thick and pulpy, like most paper these days, recycled countless times through hand-powered paper recycling machines, only to be recycled again once another case officially closed. It was an archaic practice, one that few agencies still employed, but George agreed that the pages gave their final review files a sense of credibility that only tradition could produce. George looked over the pages, then he stapled them together and stamped in red ink his personal seal in a box printed on the front page. He signed on a line within the seal, added it to the top of the file, and then slid the file into a narrow, locked bin at the side of his cubicle.

Bells chimed through a loud speaker.

"Your work day is now over," a cheerful yet soothing female voice announced. "Corporate appreciates your productivity. Thank you for working at Law-Corp."

George shut down his computer and locked his file cabinet. He would get a new stack of files in the morning, but those he had not finished today would be under lock and key until tomorrow, when they found their way to the top of his pile. George sat as the maze of thin hallways set by the cubicles became flooded with tired workers. Slowly, the people filed out.

George grabbed his lunch pail and found his way through the long room, to the stairwell that was still backed up with the flood of people filing down to the shuttle garage. George shuffled along the end of the line, moving down the stairs as a few other stragglers came in behind him. He moved in line down a staircase, until he made his way to an underground garage. He took a seat on a bench in front of the Line 150 shuttle track, wondering if it was going to be late again. The shuttles always seemed to break down when the weather was bad, and it had been raining especially heavy.

William, George's neighbor across the hall and a criminal defense manager for Law-Corp, found a seat at the end of George's bench. "Hey, George, how'd the day treat you?"

"Just fine. And you?"

"Can't complain. Just the same, I'm glad tomorrow's Friday."

George gave a knowing nod. He tolerated William well enough, although he found the man to be rather long-winded and dull. William came from money, as had his wife. Neither was exceptionally bright, and their family connections were likely all that kept either in the Corp Segregate. Still, they were the most tolerable people in the complex and it was never a bad thing to have friends who knew people in high Corporate places.

George sighed, looking down the tunnels for any sign that their shuttle was on its way. Other shuttles came and left, and still Line 150 was nowhere to be seen. "With what Trans-Corp charges, you'd think they would be on time every once in a while, eh?"

"You'd think."

The men took turns shaking their heads in disgust when the Line 150 shuttle came tearing into the garage. The sudden, heavy brakes sent it to a screeching halt, causing both men to jump to their feet. Neither took a step forward, knowing something was amiss.

The shuttle doors sprang open, and half a dozen gun-toting deviants fanned out. Everyone in the vicinity hit the ground as one of them shot into the ceiling, crying out: "Listen up, you Corporate sons of bitches!"

Most deviants could almost pass for normal humans, if it were not for their eyes. Not even contact lenses could dull the eerie, almost reflective, telltale crystalline blue sheen that easily gave their kind away. Gave George the creeps. Why scientists in the eighties had conducted the genetic experiments was beyond him, especially since they'd proven fruitless.

Deviants, descendants of those who had been the products of germ-line genetic manipulation, only had a slightly higher resistance to infections than most normal humans. Ultimately, because they'd failed to halt disease progression, and even worse, they tended to have relatively smaller brains than their unaltered counterparts, Corporate deemed their genetic makeup a failure. Because of their assumed inferior intelligence levels, deviants were allocated into the manual labor division of the Mart Segregate. They were seen rarely on this end of the district.

George and William huddled behind their bench, hoping they might go ignored.

"Everybody stay down and do what you're told, and nobody will get hurt!" the apparent leader of the deviant group screamed. "I want into Law-Corp! I need to see a file!"

No one responded.

The deviant pointed his gun at William's head.

"You look like a manager! On your feet!"

William slowly got up, putting his arms in the air. "I work in Defense! I'm one of the good guys!" The color from his face went nearly sheet white as he stared at the gun's barrel. His entire body shook. "We can talk about this without a gun pointed at my head, eh?"

The deviant didn't move. He eyed William's keys. "You can get me into the file room!" His commanding voice, amplified by the gun in his hands, did nothing to change the fact that he obviously had no understanding of the inner workings of a Corp establishment.

William's face glistened as he broke into a sudden, heavy sweat. "It doesn't work that way. I don't have those keys!"

"Then tell me who does!" The deviant charged a few steps toward William, his gun still aimed to kill.

"I don't know!" William cried, his arms waving in front of him as if they might divert a potential bullet. "Please don't shoot me!"

Everyone turned as an armored Police-Corp shuttle shot into the garage, lights rolling, and gracefully slid to a halt behind the hijacked Line 150 shuttle. William fell to his knees and closed his eyes when an officer fearlessly exited the shuttle and shot the deviant in the head.

Another deviant turned to aim at the officer, only to be shot as well. The rest, watching the squad of officers filing out and taking aim, quickly dropped their weapons and surrendered themselves.

William lowered even further, placing his hands on the cold cement ground. He took deep breaths, working to compose himself.

George hurried to his side. "Are you okay?"

William nodded.

"It's always deviants, whenever you hear about a crime," George muttered, watching the police associates drag the two bodies into the shuttle. The other four deviants stood in a circle, handcuffed, cursing their misfortune. George helped William to his feet.

William gave him a grateful nod. "I wonder what that was about."

"I don't think they need a reason," George said, perking up as a few of the officers began to clear the Line 150 shuttle.

There were bodies inside. The officers donned rubber gloves and paper booties then dragged out three bloodied security associates and a shuttle manager. Obviously, they had not let the deviants hijack the empty shuttle without a fight. It was no wonder the Police-Corp shuttle had arrived so quickly. Very likely, the altercation had begun at the shuttle's previous stop. Perhaps this had even been an organized effort, with more locations than just Law-Corp being targeted.

Both men watched in horror as a crew of sanitation associates came in to clean the shuttle. They took their time, and when they finally left, their mops and rags were stained a dark, muddy red. William became hysterical when it came time to board.

"You can't just stay here," George said.

"I just need a minute!"

"The shuttle will be gone in a minute." George grabbed William by the jacket and began to drag him in. William crumpled to a mass on the steel floor as George pulled him toward a row of empty seats.

William scrambled to a seat beside George, visibly shaking as the doors shut and the shuttle zipped out of the garage.

"You need to get a handle on yourself," George said with a concerned frown.

"I know . . . I don't know what's come over me!"

"The world didn't come to an end. A group of deviants happened to get their hands on a few firearms." George slapped William on the back, dismayed at the size of William's flinch. "A harrowing experience to impress your friends with, hey?"

William shrugged. He stared straight ahead, his lip quivering as he fell frozen in a moment of flashback. George turned to the window, pretending not to notice, watching instead the rain beating down against the shuttle windows. Visibility beyond the rain was close to zero.

"I need a good, stiff drink," William finally said.

George rolled his eyes. The snob in William was capable of coming out even in times of total crisis. With resources as scarce as they were, alcohol had become a rare commodity. Not many people had the money to throw away on something so unnecessary.

"And I wish we weren't eating out tonight," William uttered with newfound wretchedness. "I'm supposed to meet Judith at the Food-Mart."

"Maybe you should just go home. I'm sure she'll get the picture when you don't show up."

William shook his head. "I can't just leave her there. It's a long walk back from the Food-Mart to

Housing, you know."

"Then pick her up and escort her safely through the tunnels, like you've done a million times before."

The shuttle began to slow as it neared their district Housing. George stood, glad that the craziness to his day was about to end, bracing against the inertia of the massive shuttle slowing.

William fell into a panic, his body twitching and shaking as giant sobs began to escape him. "I can't do this!"

"People are looking at you," George whispered.

"I think I'm having one of those . . . you know, mental breakdowns!" William chuckled between sobs. "I can't breathe!" He began to hyperventilate.

George gave a frustrated huff. "Just get off and go home. Give Virginia a holler and tell her I went to pick up Judith for you, okay?"

William's face went wild with relief and gratitude. "You'd do that for me? Oh, you're a good friend—a *good* friend!"

The shuttle came to a halt at Housing, and George watched William scurry away, reiterating his thanks until the doors snapped closed and the shuttle was on its way to the Food-Mart.

# Chapter Two

Judith looked angry when George finally found her. The temperature in the tunnels had dropped below freezing with dusk, and she stood by the heat of a floodlight, shivering beneath her thick coat. She gave George a sideways glance as he approached her. "I didn't expect to see you here," she said, not quite looking at him.

"William sent me."

"Please don't tell me I waited all this time in the cold only for my husband to stand me up," she growled.

"There was a . . . well, an incident at the Law-Corp garage. William almost got shot by a deviant. Freaked him out a little. He sent me to walk you home."

She crossed her arms, making a show of her protest. "I stayed out here for a good meal, and a good meal is what I'm going to get! What do you feel like, Chinese or Mexican? Or maybe Mexanese?"

George shook his head. "Virginia's got pork chops waiting for me at home."

"Fine. I'll get a to-go bag from the Fast Food-

Mart," Judith said. George followed as she stormed toward the large main building.

The Restaurant Division of Food-Mart was much like any shopping mall, and was one of few establishments licensed to stay open past dusk. Most buildings, fitted with solar panels and windmills, could only generate enough electricity to keep lit for part of the day. No longer supplemented by local nuclear or water-powered generators, the energy crisis had hit its peak and then stayed there. George had barely been old enough to remember when Corporate had reduced the people's allocations, telling them that there was no longer enough energy for them to be able to use it day and night.

A typical home only had enough energy to offset the extreme temperatures, light a few rooms for a few hours before sunrise or after sunset, and cook one small meal. Most businesses lost all electrical power at dusk. Transportation-Corp began to shut down its services shortly thereafter, running only commuter shuttles until seven, and then keeping minimal lines open for the Police- and Medical-Corps until dawn.

George followed Judith to the fried chicken line.

"I should probably get something for William," Judith mumbled. "Of course, it will probably be really cold by the time I get it home."

"I'm sure he won't mind," George said, indifferent. He jumped with a start as a deviant bumped into him, grabbing his jacket to keep from tripping over and falling to the floor. With a smile, the deviant turned around and took off.

"Hey!" George turned to grab the lanky young man, but he disappeared in the crowd of people.

Judith glanced over with an annoyed huff. "Some people!"

George dug into his inside pocket, relieved to find that his wallet was still intact.

Judith got to the front counter and ordered two dinner combinations, and an apathetic food associate handed her a ticket with a number on it.

"Your bags?" the associate asked.

Judith looked at the associate for a moment, and then dug into her coat pockets with a sudden look of realization. She pulled out two folded up burlap bags and handed them over the counter.

"Thank you," said the associate, gesturing to the credit reader.

Judith zipped her credit card through the reader, and then she and George moved aside to wait for her number to come up. The line suddenly became extremely long.

Judith smiled. "Looks like we got here just in time."

George watched a few people who waited alongside them while they listened for a food associate to call Judith's number. Judith moved closer to the counter as the people walked away with their bags of greasy food. She impatiently looked at her ticket.

Judith was only a secretary for Medical-Corp, but she somehow managed to dress like a high-level manager. She wore an expensive full-length coat, covering a long, finely embroidered skirt and black, short-heeled boots that made her almost as tall as George. She had perfectly guided make-up, with flawless red lips and subtly defined eyes, and she wore her dark hair back in a tight bun. She looked smarter and much more interesting than she actually was.

Judith moved to the counter as her number blared through a loud speaker, and she traded her ticket for two bags and two large sodas. She carefully balanced the entire load in her tiny arms, and then handed the cold drinks to George. She turned to the tunnel entrance that led to Housing.

George immediately understood why Judith had handed the drinks to him, the cold air combined with the icy cups numbing his fingers. He noted Judith's quick pace and hurried to keep up with her.

"That was really nice of you to walk me home," Judith said, staying just a few steps ahead of him.

George nodded. "Sure."

Judith dug into one of the bags and began eating her French fries. "So a deviant almost shot William?"

"Yeah."

"No joke?" Judith turned to gauge George's face.

George's face was serious. "I don't miss pork chop night on account of a joke."

They continued down the tunnel, and the rain began to pound loudly overhead. The tunnels were an elaborate system that connected most of the main structures in each district. Most of the tunnels were made for pedestrian traffic, although a good number of them also shielded parts of the shuttle tracks. One could travel outside, but only when the weather permitted, and that was rare these days.

The sounds of precipitation overhead grew louder and heavier, and George looked up as if the ceiling might collapse with the deluge. "Man, it's really coming down," he said.

"Can you believe they're having a drought just fifty miles away?" Judith said with another huff.

"That's got to be an exaggeration."

She looked around to see if there was anyone nearby who might overhear her words. "I've seen pictures," she finally said, keeping her voice low. "My father works for Info-Corp. You wouldn't believe the things that don't reach the *associates*." She put her first finger over her mouth. "We don't tell too many people, so if you could keep it our little secret?"

George nodded. He cleared his throat. "Of course."

By the time they reached Housing, the cups in George's hands had gone soft with condensation and Judith's bags of food were greasy and cold. George handed the cups to William as soon as his door opened, and then he went across the hall to his humble but cozy apartment.

Tired and cold, George found a light on in the kitchen. Virginia sat, her untouched dinner sitting before her. George's dinner waited for him beside hers. "I waited for you," she said in her sweet, soft voice.

George sat down, seeing that the kids' plates had already been cleared. "Sorry I'm late."

She nodded. She took a bite of processed pork, prompting him to try his. She had blond hair that she kept long, often tying it into a loose ponytail over one shoulder. She was a patient and thoughtful woman, and even after so many years of marriage, she never failed to stir a feeling of deep contentment in him every time she smiled. And he thought her canned, reconstituted pork chops were amazing, even after sitting on the table for two hours.

"I had a long day," he said, the pork chops helping him to forget about the numerous events that had complicated his evening thus far.

"So I heard," she said, trying the room-temperature garlic-mashed potatoes. "You want to talk about it?"

He shook his head, "no."

"Well, my day was the same as usual." She got a strained look to her face, as if she were drudging up a willfully discarded memory. "The women at the office are all such nosey gossips. It's like working in an Info-Corp circle on a slow day."

"You're lucky if that's the worst of it." George took off his heavy jacket, the outside chill finally having left him. He laid his jacket over the back of his chair, too spent to go all the way to the hallway closet and hang it where it belonged.

Virginia noticed the time and got up to turn out the light. The faint glow from the wall heater was suddenly all that lit the room. Virginia had gotten counting their nighttime wattage allotment down to a science, so rarely did they suffer the steep restriction penalties.

"Did you know that Judith's father works for Info-Corp?" George asked through the darkness.

She made her way back to her seat. "Really?"

"You can't tell anyone. She told me in confidence."

Virginia nodded.

The two finished their dinner despite the dark. Virginia determined that washing the dishes could wait until tomorrow, when she had more light, and so they quietly retreated to the bedroom to make love and wait for sleep to take them into another day.

Virginia fell asleep quickly, smiling, as she fell into happy dreams.

George lay in silence, contemplating the day.

# Chapter Three

Shelley and Kurt sat at the kitchen table eating peanut butter sandwiches. Virginia set a sandwich in front of George, along with a cup of stale coffee, before she sat down at the far end of the table with her own cold breakfast.

Fifteen-year-old Shelley was tall and thin, a natural blonde with dark blue eyes. Human blue was far different from deviant blue, and luckily hers fell on the darker end of the scale. If they were dark, there was no question. Shelley fit in well at school, excelling both academically and socially, but between her friends and her schoolwork, she had little time to herself.

Seven-year-old Kurt, a lanky boy sporting glasses and freckles, squirmed in his chair, displeased that George had left his jacket along the back of it the night before. Kurt was smart, and he often played the entire family with his dark brown eyes, as everyone knew that brown-eyed boys had the most potential. Watching for a reaction, Kurt tugged at the back of George's jacket and sent the entire thing to the floor in a bulky mass.

When George failed to react, Virginia shot up from her seat and picked up the jacket. "Is it that hard to pick up after yourselves?" she scolded as she left the room with the jacket folded over her arm. She noticed something hitting against her from the front outside pocket as she went for the closet, and she dug her hand in to find an unusual business card.

A light dusting of blue glitter came off onto her fingertips as Virginia tried to discern what appeared to be a coded message on one side. Unable to read it, she hung up the jacket and returned to the kitchen.

George had scarfed down his sandwich and was finishing his coffee as Virginia came back. He noticed the sparkling card in her hand. "What's that?"

"You don't recognize it? I found it in your jacket pocket."

George got up, eyeing the card as he passed her. "Probably some kind of promotional or movement act advertisement. Go ahead and toss it."

She nodded. "Meet you in the shower."

He hurried down the hall with a smile, closing the bathroom door behind him as he entered, shedding his nightclothes as he waited for the water to heat up. As he entered, he realized that he had set the water hotter than he should have, but then decided that he would wait and cool it off in a minute or two. The hot water felt good against his back. Hot water used a great deal of energy, regardless of whether or not the water recycler was on, and so George turned down the heat before steam could accumulate on the mirror. Virginia always had a comment for him if she saw steam. He washed and rinsed quickly, then waited for

Virginia with the water recycler on at full power. After several minutes, he called out, "Virginia, are you coming?"

Virginia finally entered, throwing off her bathrobe and hurrying from the cold, tile bathroom to the lukewarm shower. She turned off the water recycler. "I can't get this damn glitter off," she said with great frustration as she motioned for George to vacate the shower.

He took the hint and grabbed his towel, slipping out as she hurried beneath the hot water. He watched from aside as she rinsed and scrubbed her hands, only spreading the glitter up her arms and onto the soap.

"What a mess!" she said. "Guess I know what I'm doing when I get off work this afternoon."

George dried off and got dressed as Kurt began to knock persistently at the door.

"Shelley hit me!"

"Did not!"

George slid out of the room, slamming the door behind him as the two children stared back. "Can't you two get along for one morning?"

"But she—"

"I don't want to hear it! Both of you, finish getting ready!"

Both showed a look of protest, but neither said another word as they retreated to their rooms. George returned to the bathroom to comb his hair, surprised to find Virginia still scrubbing her glittery, powder blue hands. "You're going to miss your shuttle," he said.

She nodded, too preoccupied respond any further.

"I'm walking Kurt to his shuttle station now. I'll

see you tonight." He blew her a kiss.

She nodded again as he left her to her shower.

VIRGINIA TOOK the Line 210 shuttle every morning, which delivered her right to the doorstep at Communications-Corp. The weather delayed the shuttle over a half hour just before her stop, and yet she still received a demerit for her late arrival to work. The garage was unusually crowded when her shuttle came in. She didn't have the time to get a closer look, but it seemed as though a group of Mart-level employees was having another demonstration. Security associates were everywhere, and so far, the event looked peaceful. Virginia knew that once the horn blew, matters would get ugly, however, as it was a corporate offense to miss one's shift intentionally. She hurried to the Communications Building, not wanting to become caught in the crowd.

Virginia worked in residential telephone communications, which was mostly restricted to workers in the Corp Segregate. There were phones in Mart housing districts, but generally they were only used for emergencies because of their cost. Cell phones had long ago been abandoned throughout the region because of constant blackouts from the weather, but landline communications had also suffered a significant blow. The cost of maintenance was substantial, and so it was kept to a minimum. At any given time, lines were down somewhere in the district. As with transportation, communication between even nearby districts was well beyond the scope of most people's incomes and thus almost nonexistent.

Virginia made her way to the call room, the building so cold that she opted to keep her jacket tightly wrapped around her and her gloves and hat on. She sat down at her station, trying to get comfortable in her headset. As a call center associate, Virginia had only a switchboard, a policy manual, and an electronic pen and notepad. All complaints she could not handle went to the call center manager, a fat, grumpy old man named Robert who often raised his voice loud enough for the associates to be able to hear him through the wall to his office. Robert didn't seem to mind dealing with one irate customer after another. In fact, he seemed to thrive on the conflict. Virginia couldn't stand the man.

The bulk of today's complaints came from people who lived in the upper west end of the district, all calling from their corner-office telephones because they had gone without their personal communication lines since yesterday. Yesterday's storm had destroyed a couple of main circuits that fed the lines, and it seemed that the repair associates were the low level employees organizing that strike out in the garage. They contended that they weren't making enough money to compensate for the elements they faced each day, and unless they were paid more and were given Housing upgrades, they would be making no more communications repairs.

Virginia forwarded every complaint to Robert. One could only hope that a sufficient number of repair associates would be cut a big enough deal to be back at work and have the lines up and running soon. That would be the best-case scenario; the worst-case scenario would involve people dying in the garage.

Virginia hoped she wouldn't have to see any bodies. The workers did have a valid complaint, but their means of complaining was illegal and the law did not allow for excuses, no matter how valid they were.

Zelda, a thin woman with dark features sitting two chairs down from Virginia, put a man on hold and threw her headset onto the desk. She turned to Jane, a plump woman sitting between her and Virginia, as she put her hand to her forehead in a melodramatic display, and feigned, "I can't take it anymore!" She chuckled, her head nudging toward an empty seat on the other side of the room.

Jane giggled with her.

The seat across the room had been vacant for a few days now, after Carolyn, a young woman who had been hired fresh out of school just shy of a year ago, experienced a mental breakdown. She threw her headset down onto the desk, clearly after having transferred an especially difficult call to Robert, and then screamed about how unbearable the system was until the security associates came. It took three of them to drag her, hysterical and screaming, out of the building. She had been a sweet girl up until then. What became of her, no one knew. What all the women did know, however, was that Corporate held her seat unfilled for a reason. It was there to remind them of what became of those who could not handle their simple jobs.

Virginia was old enough to remember life just when Corporate America was beginning to take hold. A free market system was still in place, although privately owned shops and other small businesses slowly fell to the wayside as superstores and giant corporations smothered them all, one by one. The free market system dissolved as monopolies took over. Those in power took advantage of what they could, knowing there was no stopping the monster, and soon the delineation between the monopolies and the government became close to indistinguishable.

Shortly after free trade disappeared internationally, the Big Climate Change reached critical mass. For roughly a decade, the oceans rushed in on their shores, creating all new shorelines across the globe, and hurricanes and tornadoes tore across several states at a time. While the bulk of Europe turned into swamp and marshland, most of Asia became arid and hot. Like Africa, both Americas became a mishmash of unpredictable weather patterns. The weather decimated those three continents, knocking out their communications with the rest of the world and forcing them to rebuild all of their countries from the ground-up.

In the United States, for the sake of efficiency and economy, communities were rebuilt into underground districts. Roughly the size of small cities, districts were grouped into quadroplexes that could be self-contained, should neighboring areas suffer structural or socioeconomic hardship. Which district in a quadroplex one lived in was determined by where one worked, and where one worked depended upon where one's family worked: typically, Corps begot Corps and Marts begot Marts.

Core governments still had small amounts of communication between them, but the Internet no longer existed. Even the closest of family living in different regions eventually lost touch. Further destruction ensured that communications among most districts dissolved as well, and the people slowly learned to accept their isolation.

Livestock became increasingly difficult to keep, and before long, large grazers like cattle completely disappeared. Many species of fish went extinct, and the price of pork and chicken nearly tripled. Fresh food was rare. The variety of available fruits and vegetables became limited by region, although the majority of farms now grew genetically modified crops beneath enormous Plexiglas domes.

Virginia remembered when houses sat on open lots, when people were allowed to have pets, and when a person could take a long, hot shower without receiving a hefty fine. Much had changed throughout her lifetime, and not for the better. When she was a child, life seemed to be all about getting ahead while shamelessly living beyond one's means. Most Americans consumed excessively, were spoiled by outrageous advances in technology, and left countless landfills with what should have been renewable resources. Now, life was a matter of survival. Everything was expensive. Everything had to be recycled. Waste was just an old American pipe dream.

The system was depressing, but there was not much one could do about it beyond showing up for work every day and doing one's job. What kept Virginia going was the knowledge that her children would have the opportunity, should they do well enough in school, to find themselves in ruts just a little less monotonous than hers.

By the time the lunch chimes sounded, no one in

the call center was paying much attention to their calls and Robert's switchboard was flooded.

Dozens of box lunches came out, and the women in the call center moved around leisurely as they ate sandwiches and canned fruits. Virginia found peanut butter was not appetizing enough today, and she closed her lunch box and set it aside for later.

Jane moved to her desk and leaned against it, sipping cold coffee. "You okay?"

Virginia nodded, although she was feeling a little tired.

"You look kind of pale," Jane said.

Virginia smiled. "I'm fine . . . really."

# Chapter Four

Shelley stuck close to her small group of friends as they moved on foot from the shuttle garage to the beach. Her parents had taken her and Kurt to the beach before, but because of the expense, the weather, and the long hike out, the family had only gone a couple of times. Going to a place like the beach with her friends, where the air felt clean and there was nothing looming beyond but sand dunes and a vast, grey ocean, somehow enabled her to breathe a little easier than she usually did. The fact that she was going without her parents' knowledge made the trip both worrisome and exhilarating.

The clouds lumbered overhead, threatening. It had not rained all day, but the ground was still wet and soft from last night's deluge. Shelley realized early into the hike that the thick mud was destroying her sneakers. Everyone in the group seemed to be sharing her tough luck, and she was thankful that she had opted not to wear her dress flats. She had considered it in a brief, clouded moment of vanity, but luckily, she had come to her senses when she considered the length of the planned hike. She noticed that her friend Charlotte had not.

Charlotte had flaming red hair and a thick distribution of freckles on her pale face. Her green eyes had a recklessness to them that depicted a past about which she talked very little. She carried her short heels in one hand, moving barefoot through the cold mud. Her face showed a combination of disgust and determination as she struggled to lead the small group.

Three other teenagers, two boys and a girl, followed close behind. Shelley was not very close with any of them, although she did see them often at school. Charlotte didn't seem to like them much either, but she did like the attention they gave her. The other girl was short, with green eyes, a black bob, and painfully crooked teeth. The two boys were both tall, one of them towering over the other. Both had dark eyes and sandy blond hair.

The group moved cautiously through the sand, and still a pair of police associates riding mountain bikes from the opposing direction caught them off-guard. A loud whistle caused the group to stop where they were, and the police associates rolled to a stop beside them.

"ID cards!" one of the associates barked, and the kids scrambled to find their cards.

Shelley found her ID card and handed it to the police associate. "We're just headed to the beach."

"You know beach property is closed after sunset?" the officer asked while scanning Shelley's card in a small, hand-held computer. He glanced at the sun, which now barely hovered over the mountains.

Shelley nodded.

With his computer showing no warrants on Shelley, the police associate handed her card back to her. "Don't let me catch you out here after hours."

Shelley pocketed the ID. "You won't."

"There is a new shantytown of deviants living in the district right above us," the police associate continued. "There have been reports that they're spreading down closer to us, even roaming our beaches at night. You don't want to get mugged, do you?"

Shelley shook her head.

The officers checked the rest of the group's ID cards and then, after giving the group one last warning about the deviants and beach policies, they continued on their way.

There was a biting chill to the windy beach air, and yet everyone in the group abandoned their shoes as they approached the soft, fine sand. Shelley looked around. "I don't know if this was such a good idea," she said, noticing a new front of clouds prematurely darkening the horizon.

"We must be a little early," Charlotte said, looking unsure of what else to say. All eyes were suddenly on her. She cleared her throat, getting visibly nervous. "They'll be here."

Shelley felt herself grow increasingly nervous as the minutes passed. She had never met Charlotte's new friends, but she knew some of their reputations. They had a steady source of bootleg liquor, however, and Shelley's curiosity over the intoxicant temporarily outweighed all reason in her decision-making skills. Still, she knew she was there to break the law, and she knew the potential repercussions. She gave an impatient huff. "They're not coming. We should get out of here."

"They'll be here," Charlotte insisted.

Shelley crossed her arms. "I really think—"

She fell silent as the sound of fuel-powered motors swept in from the distance.

Everyone watched in silence as a dust cloud from the north slowly grew to become three sand-cruisers. The loud and clumsy machines carried three young men in their late teens to early twenties swiftly across the beach. The motors were loud and smelly, putting out huge amounts of exhaust, and the propulsion systems polluted the air with the jets of sand the vehicles left in their wake. They had been outlawed after the automotive unit for Transportation-Corp was shut down, and so their use clearly defined their riders as outlaws. In patches where the sand was dry, the sand-cruisers kicked up tall clouds of dust, giving the appearance of smoke plumes from a shoreline fire.

The three young men came to a halt in front of the group and turned off their engines.

"Change of plans. We're meeting in District 89148 tonight. Hop on," one of them said. He patted the back seat of his sand-cruiser. He had multiple piercings and visible tattoos, and his hair was multiple shades of red and orange.

"Where are we going?" Shelley asked, afraid to move.

"To a party," the young man said with a chilling smile. "There'll be plenty of cigarettes and alcohol, and maybe even some food."

Charlotte sprang over to the vehicle and sat down

behind the young man. The rest of the group looked among one another, not sure what to do. The girl and the taller of the boys joined Charlotte and her friends, but Shelley and the second boy remained uncertain.

"You're not going to chicken out now, are you?" Charlotte asked as the group started their engines.

"I'm cold . . . and it's getting dark," Shelley said, backing from the sand cruisers.

"Suit yourself," the young man said. Whipping up a six-foot arc of sand at Shelley, he spun the vehicle around and then took off, returning to the north. The two other drivers followed suit, and soon the three were nothing but a hum and a low haze vanishing in the distance.

Shelley and her companion stared off into the horizon until there was nothing left to see, and then they turned one another, dazed.

*And what of Charlotte?*

"We should start walking," Shelley said.

At her prompt, the two began their long trek back to the shuttle garage.

In what felt like a vindictive act of God, it began to rain. It came just a few drops at a time at first, but within just a few minutes, the two hiked through heavy sheets of water. The rain quickly grew cold and relentless, and visibility went to nothing.

Water began to pool all over the muddy ground, and as the two sloshed through it, their clothes grew filthy and ragged. Their bare feet became cold and raw. Still, they continued on, having no nearby shelter in which to wait out the storm. Dark clouds blanketed the sky, and lightning began to crash far off in the north.

# Chapter Five

Virginia made chicken nuggets and vegetables on Fridays. She set the table late, having expected Shelley home with her school shuttle. The girl had disappeared with her friends before, so the family did not worry about her as much as they groaned over a delayed dinner. By the time the sun set, Kurt and George both began complaining about how hungry they were, and the three sat down and ate without her. Virginia cleared the table, then sat and waited.

When eight o'clock came, she reluctantly turned out the kitchen light. She returned to her seat at the kitchen table, the glow of the wall heater turning her into a silhouette before Kurt's and George's dimly lit faces. She turned to Kurt. "Time to get ready for bed."

Kurt got up, but remained by his seat. "I don't want to go."

"Mommy's tired," she said.

"But the bathroom and the hallway are dark, and if there's a monster in my room, I wouldn't know it was there." Kurt looked over at George. "Daddy, will you sit with me while I brush my teeth?"

George got to his feet. "Sure, buddy."

The two filed out of the room, and the faint glow from the bathroom's battery-powered click-light seeped into the dark hall.

Virginia stayed close to the heater, the chill getting the best of her. It was likely twenty degrees colder outside. If Shelley didn't get home soon, she could freeze to death.

Virginia closed her eyes as the room began to spin. She took a deep breath, knowing her anxiety was getting the best of her. Shelley was a smart, resourceful young woman, and she needed the room to test her wings, as hard as it was to let her do. She felt her body go flush, and she began to shiver in a sudden cold sweat. Struggling against an onset of nausea, she got to her feet, went to her room, pulled off her shirt, and then collapsed into bed.

George and Kurt finished up in the bathroom, and then George walked Kurt to his room. He turned off the light and found his way into his bedroom. Virginia gathered the blankets over her body as another chill raced through her.

"I'm going to wait up a while longer." George said moved to give Virginia a kiss on the forehead. "You're burning up."

"I thought I felt something coming on earlier today," she said, shivering. "I heard there's a flu going around," she added, although she had heard nothing of the sort. "I'm so cold. Lie down with me for just a minute?"

George got in bed, turning his back to her. "Don't

40

give it to me."

"My apologies in advance if I do," she said, nestling her sweaty back up against his to offset the chill.

George moved to get comfortable. The temperature under the covers was smothering, but the bedroom was so cold that George could almost see his breath. He tried to adjust the blankets to find a reasonable temperature, and Virginia tugged at them with another shiver, shifting them to favor her side. He sighed, resigning himself to the idea that, if his insomnia did not keep him awake tonight, Virginia surely would.

At least tomorrow was Saturday.

Most people who worked in the Corp Segregate, George and Virginia included, rarely worked on weekends. On Saturdays, Kurt helped himself to dry cereal and comic books, while George and Virginia slept in until around nine and Shelley stayed in bed until at least noon. The bulk of most Sundays were devoted to church functions, although George and Virginia both agreed that Faith-Corp's district sermon manager was egotistical and short-fused. Unfortunately, one could not simply stop going to church because of personal issues. Everyone went to church.

Virginia often joked that they might as well go every week to get their tithing's worth. Faith-Corp had somehow contracted them into monthly payments by direct deposit, and everyone knew better than to tangle with the church's high-paid Law-Corp managers. Faith-Corp also knew whenever George and Virginia had opted to let their family sleep in on a

Sunday, bombarding them with visits by associates from the church council, stressing the importance of attendance. It was simply easier to go, even if church had become just a Corporate shell of what George and Virginia remembered it to be.

Most people in their segregate weren't old enough to remember what George and Virginia remembered, though, and among them, the majority had long ago forgotten God. There were enough enormous entities to fear and worship these days without adding Him into the mix.

Virginia rolled over with a moan as she continued to lie restlessly in bed. Sweat poured from her and heat emanated from her skin, and yet she could not will her body to stop shivering. Her back began to tense up, and she stretched and contorted in an attempt to alleviate her growing discomfort.

She struggled to reorient herself as a wave of nausea hit her. She got to her feet and hurried down the dark hall. She coughed and retched over the toilet until a thick, bitter liquid came. She sat where she was for a moment, barely able to move. When she finally did try to stand, her legs failed her before she could take a single step. She crumpled to the linoleum, her head smacking against the hard floor, and then the dark room faded into a senseless black void.

GEORGE HEARD the sickening thump Virginia's head made when it hit the linoleum, and he sat up. "What was that?"

"Daddy?" Kurt cried out.

George rushed into Kurt's room. "Kurt?"

Kurt hid beneath his covers. "Daddy, I heard a monster in the bathroom."

George hurried to the bathroom and activated the little light. Virginia lay unconscious on the floor. "Virginia?"

The telephone sat amidst a few other rarely used items on a shelf across in the living room. George stumbled through the darkness to find it, then brought it back into the bathroom and dialed Emergency Dispatch-Corp.

An emergency associate answered on the third ring. "This is Emergency. How may I direct your call?"

"My wife is unconscious," George cried. "I think she hit her head."

"All of our medical associates are out on other calls right now. Your estimated wait for a medic shuttle is three hours. Do you want me to put you on the list?"

"Three hours? She could be dead by then!"

"Do you or do you not want on the list?"

"Yes—but she needs help *now*."

"I'm sorry, sir, but three hours is the best we can do for you. If you'd like to speak to my manager, I'd be more than happy to transfer your call."

"Please do!" George yelled.

Kurt began to cry from his bedroom as light, tired music began to play into George's ear. He sat at Virginia's side, trying to wake her, ignoring Kurt's pleas for him to come back and keep him safe from his imagined monsters.

Virginia didn't move. George checked for a pulse, relieved with the reassurance that she was still alive.

Leigh M. Lane

The music continued through the telephone, one song running into another. A recording came on: "The next three minutes will cost ten-fifty. Press one to accept the charges. To forfeit press two, or simply hang up."

The front door opened and then squealed closed, and George tensed up even tighter. He hung up the telephone. "Shelley—in here!"

Shelley shuffled in, barefoot, covered in mud, her face puffy with tears. Her eyes went wide, and she collapsed down to Virginia's side. "Mom?"

"Help me get her to the bed," George said.

George got Virginia's upper body, while Shelley carried her legs. They slowly made their way to the bedroom, and then carefully laid her across the bed. She continued to sweat with her fever, and George opted to cover her only lightly.

"What happened?" Shelley asked.

George shook his head. "I don't know. She said there was a flu going around."

"Shouldn't she go to the hospital?" Shelley continued backing up until she got to the door.

"I tried. Everyone's busy."

"But this is an emergency!"

"It doesn't matter. No one's coming to help," George yelled. "And where the hell have you been?"

Shelley looked down. "I got lost."

George was in no mood to argue with her, so he simply nodded and turned away.

The thought occurred to him that he and Shelley together might be able to carry Virginia to the hospital, and then he considered that the medic shuttle would probably get there before they were able to reach the hospital on foot. He thought to call Emergency again, but thought better of it.

"Virginia?" he tried, giving her shoulder a gentle nudge. When she did not respond, grief swelled up in him and he couldn't help but cry aloud.

There was nothing he could do at that moment but lie next to her and hold her as tightly as he could. He wrapped his arms around her, helpless.

"Daddy, *please* come in here!" Kurt cried from his bedroom. "I'm scared! The monsters!"

# Chapter Six

Virginia woke to the frightening realization that she was not in her own bed. She opened her eyes and the room slowly came into focus. She was in the hospital. There was an intravenous needle in her arm, and fluids dripped from a bag hanging over her head. She lay in a tiny isolation room with layers of clear, split plastic walls between her and the locked door. A camera watched her.

She tried to sit up, but every muscle in her body burned and ached. She looked into the camera. "Hello! Somebody?"

She tried to think back to her last memory. Her head throbbed and her thoughts were fuzzy, but she was able to recall being in the bathroom. She had gotten sick. A black sheet had enveloped her, smothering out her thoughts, when she had tried to stand up from the toilet.

*How long had she been unconscious?*

She began to panic. She pulled the needle from her arm and forced her legs over the side of the bed.

Ignoring the burning and weakness in her muscles, she willed herself to sit up. She slowly got to her shaky feet, fatigue tearing through her body as she struggled to hold her weight. A medical associate and his manager, both clad in biological protection suits, burst into the room.

"Calm down, Ma'am!" the manager said.

"Where am I?"

"Medical-Corp, District Hospital," the manager said. "Don't worry. You're going to be okay."

The men helped her back into the bed, and the associate recovered the intravenous needle hanging off the side. A small pool of saline collected on the linoleum, but both doctors ignored it. They seemed far too concerned with making sure Virginia stayed in bed and had the needle back in her arm.

"How long was I out?" she asked.

"A little over twelve hours," the associate said.

"Where's my family?"

"We'll need to keep you in isolation for a few days," the manager answered. "Whatever virus is going around, it's a nasty one, and we need to contain it."

"Can I get you some reading materials?" the associate asked. "Something to help pass the time?"

The room suddenly seemed even smaller. Virginia felt her body trickle with more sweat, the cold chills threatening to return. "There isn't any way I can just go home?"

The two men exchanged glances, and then the manager replied, "You'll only be here for a few days at the most, I'm sure. There's really nothing I can do about it. I'll voice your concerns to my manager, though, if you want me to."

"Don't bother," Virginia grumbled, knowing the system all too well.

"Here." The manager emptied a syringe that seemed to have come from nowhere into Virginia's arm. "A little something for the pain."

"But I don't want—" Everything became a blur, and suddenly Virginia didn't care that she was being held against her will under monitored confinement. She didn't care that most people who stayed in these small rooms only left after a date with the euthanasia machine. She didn't even care that the rest of her family could easily end up sharing her uncertain fate. Nothing mattered now but the numbing bliss that pulsed through her veins.

She didn't see the medical associate and manager leave the room. She was too busy watching little imaginary bugs scurrying across the ceiling. There were colors, too, yellows and violets moving in odd shapes and patterns, as if she were gazing through a kaleidoscope. The pain throughout her body vanished, and Virginia decided that the manager who injected it wasn't quite as terrible as she had first assessed.

She closed her eyes and watched the drug induced show, content enough for the time being. Everything slowly became dull, fading to black, and she lay in a mindless fog for longer than she could measure. Her mind took her to a field of wild poppies. The air was fragrant instead of wet and grey, and there wasn't a building or shuttle track in sight. Virginia smiled. There were no more walls. They had dissolved with her headache. There was no more hospital. There was just her and an endless field.

To her surprise, one of the poppies in front of her turned to the poppy beside it. "She'll be out for at least another hour," it began, speaking in the medical associate's voice.

"Go ahead and bring in the students," another poppy said in the manager's commanding voice.

All of the poppies surrounding Virginia turned to face her.

Virginia could hear the clicking of shoes on a hard floor, but the only movement she saw was the field of poppies rippling with the breeze.

"This patient has been kept in a sedated state for three days, and this morning she was listed non-contagious," the manager poppy said. "We've taken DNA samples, however, and unfortunately hers has turned out the same as all of the rest."

All of the poppies stared in on her as a bright light came from nowhere and shone straight into her face. She tried to turn away, her eyes watering from the light, and suddenly she realized that she was in the hospital room, surrounded by people in white coats and facemasks, with a pocket light shining directly into one of her eyes.

Virginia sat up with a gasp, and the group around her took a collective step back. Her gaze quickly shot over to those of the manager, and then she looked at the rest of the men pleadingly. "Please don't let him sedate me again! I want to know what's going on!"

"Calm down, Ma'am."

"I want to see my husband!"

"Let's worry about one thing at a time," the manager said.

"I know my rights! You said yourself I'm not

contagious. I want my discharge papers now!" Virginia yelled.

"Your rights have changed," the manager said, letting the rest of the group know exactly where she now stood.

Virginia tried to get out of the bed. The manager gave a few of the others a subtle nod, and they swarmed in on her and pinned her down. The manager injected another potent sedative into her thigh, and she went limp almost immediately.

The medical manager turned to his senior associate. "Call Corporate and see if they've decided whether or not to declare the group dead."

The associate nodded then quickly left the room with meaning and importance to his gait.

Virginia could hear what the manager said, but she could barely keep from drooling on herself, let alone flee for her life. She stared up at the bugs and moving colors once more, praying that she might wake up to live another day, if just long enough to know what exactly she would be dying for.

# Chapter Seven

Medical-Corp sent an associate to check the rest of the family for signs of infection. The associate gave George a small box of ashes. "Our condolences."

"They said it was some kind of virus?" George asked, pulling the box close to his body.

"A retrovirus deployed somehow by a deviant terrorist group," the associate said. "As far as we can tell, the virus isn't airborne. Still, your entire family could have been exposed to the same agent that infected her, so I'm going to need to examine all of you, search your home, and take a detailed history of the past week."

George shrugged. "A history of what? It was a week, just like any other week."

The medical associate gave George a sympathetic face. "I know this is hard for you, Mr. Irwin, but I need you to think. Did your wife go anywhere or do anything new or different?"

George shook his head, barely able to think. He clutched his arms tighter around the box, shaking his head.

"Did she bring home anything unusual? Any second-hand jewelry or make-up?"

George continued to shake his head.

"Nothing painted with a kind of messy, blue glitter?"

George froze, his mind rushing back to the previous morning. "Blue glitter?" he asked, his throat going uncomfortably tight.

The associate nodded.

George fought a disorienting moment of dissociation as he struggled to recall the details of the previous morning. "There was a card. I think she threw it in the trash." He moved toward the trash compactor, but the associate stopped him. The man donned gloves and a mask, then he picked though the trash until he found the glittery card. He bagged the compactor's full contents and carefully searched the rest of the apartment, finding nothing else of interest. He gave George, Shelley, and Kurt each a quick exam, even though none of them looked sick. After giving them clean bills of health, he ordered a seventy-two-hour in-home quarantine and left the three to grieve in peace.

No one took the news of Virginia's death well, but George took it the hardest. He couldn't help but feel guilty over not having gotten Virginia to a doctor sooner. He felt partially responsible, even though he knew there was nothing else he could have done for her. He struggled to remain composed as he told Shelley and Kurt the news.

Monday was usually egg- and vegetable-fried rice night.

No one else felt up to cooking, let alone eating, so the three simply sat at the table, trying to digest the bitter fact that the cornerstone of their family would never be returning home. The evening dragged by slowly, and when George finally turned off the lights, Kurt began to sob loudly.

"I don't want to go to bed tonight, Daddy!"

George picked up Kurt and sat him on his lap. "No one has to go to bed tonight, buddy."

Kurt continued to cry, and George cried with him. Maybe this evening was all just a bad nightmare, and they would all wake up to find that Monday hadn't yet come. George would have a tiresome day at work, Shelley would get into some kind of mischief with Charlotte, and Kurt would sit in an introverted little world of his own the entire school day, but they would get home to find that Virginia had returned and everything was actually okay.

George envisioned her face in his mind's eye. Her lips, her thin curves, that trill that came to her voice when she got really excited . . . now all reduced to an ashy box on the kitchen table. Why hadn't he said anything when he had the chance? Why had he been so selfish?

Kurt finally calmed down, although he still clung to George as if he might be going next. Shelley stared at a wall.

George was not sure how much more he was going to be able to take. His own grief was profound enough, but watching his children grieve was pure agony. The wall heater switched to low. George sat Kurt with Shelley and disappeared to get a few thick blankets, needing to be alone with his thoughts for a moment. He went to his bedroom and grabbed the blanket off the bed, and then sat down and smelled Virginia's pillow for a moment. She was still there. He knew she would fade, but for now, she was still there. He wanted to close his eyes and lose himself forever in her smell, but instead he set the pillow back in its spot and left to get blankets for Shelley and Kurt.

They huddled together by the wall heater.

He watched the two sleep, wishing that he might quiet his mind long enough to get some rest, himself. He was so tired that he felt almost numb, and yet his eyes would not stay closed. He turned to the clock and watched the night slowly pass . . . by the hour, by the minute, by the second. . . .

Wrapping a blanket around him, he got to his feet and slowly moved to his bedroom. He found Virginia's pillow once more and searched for her scent. Afraid he might soil the sweet memory of her essence with his own musky odor, he made sure not to rest his head against the pillow as he curled up beside it and allowed himself another good cry.

# Chapter Eight

Virginia sat among a dozen other subjects, all of whom had been held at the hospital anywhere between three days and three weeks. The small room in which all of their beds had been crammed had clean, white walls and no windows. The lights overhead were dim and gave them a rough indication of the time, turning on at dawn, and shutting off sharply at dusk. There was no way out of the room, save the one locked door by the bathroom. The bathroom, a small, white tiled room, had multiple showerheads on one side, a half-wall barrier, and two toilets on the other side. A moderately-sized sink sat along the wall across from the toilets. There were no mirrors. A single camera swept its eye back and forth over the main room.

Virginia first suspected something was amiss when it occurred to her that everyone else in the room was a deviant. Then, a shocking revelation came to her when one of the others stood, spread his arms, stared up at the camera, and yelled, "Why am I locked in here with a bunch of *deviants?* What are you trying to prove?"

Everyone in the room turned to the man, and his eyes went wide at the unwanted attention.

"Nothing against any of you," he said, his voice suddenly low and uncertain.

"I'm not a deviant," said a young woman sitting nearby.

Everyone else watched in silence as the two stared at one another's eyes, the impossible answer suddenly becoming painfully clear: Each had entered the hospital a common human, but would be leaving as a deviant. Would Corporate even let them leave, or would the establishment keep them all for research purposes? Medical-Corp Management gave them no indication as to how the virus had been spread, but it was clear that they were being held for Corporate research.

Most of the people there became too bitter about their situation even to converse among one another. Although they were all victims of the same crime, animosity ran thick throughout the room. They were lab rats in an overcrowded cage, and already a few of them were ready to slit throats for the sake of just a little more space.

There were two people Virginia felt she could trust, a young woman named Emily and a middle-aged man named Olaf. Emily had a pretty figure, a sweet smile, and dark, straight hair. She was a cashier associate for Food-Mart's Grocery Division, and she was engaged to be married. Olaf had short salt-and-pepper hair and a long, grey beard. He worked as a manager for Housing-Corp, had a wife of almost thirty years, and had a son who worked for

Transportation-Corp. Emily and Olaf both had insight enough to realize they were in this together, and with Virginia, they discussed possible escape strategies at night, huddled behind the short wall in the bathroom.

It was morning, as they had been fed breakfast already but they had not yet been fed lunch. Virginia sat on the floor facing Emily, and the two played rummy with a flimsy, worn deck of cards. Olaf walked up and down the room, feeling out the rest of the group for potential co-conspirators. Most of them ignored him, but a couple of them grew hostile at his presence. Another older man screamed obscenities and shoved Olaf aside, while a young man threatened to knock out his teeth if he didn't stick to his side of the room.

Olaf sat down on the bed beside Virginia, his face strained. "Let the rest of them rot here," he muttered.

"I can't believe that guy threatened to punch you!" Emily said, making sure she was loud enough for the young man to hear her across the room.

"And I'll knock out your pretty little teeth, too, sweetheart!" the young man angrily yelled back.

Emily rolled her eyes, returning to her cards.

Everyone looked up as the locks on the door clicked open. A medical manager walked in carrying a briefcase, an armed security associate on either side of him. The door shut behind them, and he took a few steps toward the beds. Everyone went silent as they waited to hear what he had to say.

"We understand your situation is unfortunate, and we are doing what we can to keep all of you as comfortable as possible," the medical manager began. "There is a good possibility that we will not be able to reverse the virus' effects, I'm afraid. I hope you can understand that we can't just return you to your families . . . given the circumstances." The blank expression that suddenly took over his face was chilling as he continued. "Corporate has approved free euthanasia for any in here who request it." He opened his briefcase and removed a sign-up sheet. "I'll just need your signatures."

"Why can't we just go home?" a young woman cried from her bed. "I'm still me! I don't feel any different!"

"I'm sorry," the medical manager said. "Corporate has the final say on this, unfortunately, and Corporate still hasn't decided what we're going to do with all of you."

The young woman sprang from her bed and made a dash for the door.

The security associates blocked the young woman as if they were linebackers working against a three hundred-pound foe. They sent her flying, and her body hit the floor with a loud smack. She stayed down, crying, unable to move from the awkward position in which the throw had landed her. She fell silent after only a moment, going limp and still.

Emily moved to get up, but Olaf put a hand on her shoulder and held her back. "Choose your battles."

The room went silent as two young men and one older woman hesitantly approached the medical manager and signed his sheet. Virginia covered her mouth, positive some horrible noise might escape her lips if she didn't hold them shut. She turned away, unable to watch as one of the security associates led the three away. *How could they give up so easily?*

The medical manager left, the second security associate at his heels. The door slammed closed behind him, locking with a loud *click*.

Virginia looked over at her new friends, grateful that both of them were above simply signing their lives away. She had lost too much as of late, and she couldn't bear the thought of losing anything more.

"I can't believe they would just as soon kill us," Emily said, her eyes still on the door.

"It's probably less paperwork for them," Olaf said.

Virginia nodded in agreement, then moved to the young woman on the floor. She knelt down at the woman's side, gently putting a hand on her shoulder. "Hey . . . are you okay?"

The woman was unresponsive, but alive.

The door unlocked and opened once more, this time with two nurse associates pushing a gurney. Virginia backed away as the nurse associates charged up to the fallen woman. A security associate gruffly watched the door as the nurse associates picked up the woman, tossed her onto the gurney, and removed her from the room. The door locked with another jarring *click*, the room falling deathly silent.

Virginia looked around, the empty beds suddenly adding a strange new ambiance to the room. That the beds represented three, maybe four, dead people gave them almost a haunted feel, as if their spirits might rise up through their disheveled sheets and haunt the room from that day forward. The absence of just four people, however, did relax the room in a way Virginia did not want to admit. What had her world come to? Her mind drifted back to thoughts of her family. She had to stay strong if she ever wanted to see George and the kids again. She was determined to find a way out, back to her family.

Virginia looked up as the camera's eye passed over her. She wondered if a group of research managers in white coats was watching them, or if maybe the camera simply fed into a small, dark room where one or two low level associates of some kind stared at tiny screens and ate popcorn all day.

The camera panned to the other side of the room and Virginia turned to her friends. She found it interesting that despite them, the other remaining patients, and the camera, she could still feel so alone. She considered that everyone else in there probably felt the same.

Emily gathered up the cards and began to shuffle. Virginia and Olaf both motioned that they weren't in the mood to play, and so she set up a game of solitaire with a shrug.

# Chapter Nine

Shelley took the school shuttle past Housing to the exchange garage, where she found the direct line to the Food-Mart. Finding herself bombarded with the bulk of her mother's chores, Shelley held strong as she carried George's debit card and the burlap grocery bags through the dense shuttle crowd. Virginia had always gone shopping on Wednesdays, insisting that it was the best day of the week for all of the good sales, so Shelley too went on Wednesday.

She wore a surgical facemask and plastic gloves, as Corporate had issued a red alert. She had gone shopping with Virginia before, to learn the process, but entering Food Mart's Grocery Division on her own for the first time was still overwhelming. The colossal establishment seemed much more crowded than usual. Several lines of people wrapped around the different vending booths in confusing and erratic patterns. People pushed their way past one another. Music played over a loud speaker, helping to offset the noise created by so many people trying to speak over one another at once. Occasionally, the music would pause and a pleasant voice would take over the speaker to announce overstock specials, news associate locations, and random Corporate pearls of wisdom.

"Attention, Food-Mart customers," the voice announced. "For today only, the canned meat product booth is having a buy three, get one free sale (limit two free items). And remember, a hard worker is a happy worker. Thank you for shopping at Food-Mart."

Shelley pulled the list from her bag, struggling to orient herself as panic threatened to freeze her where she stood. She closed her eyes, took a deep breath, and began to look over the items on her list, which she had listed by booth. Virginia had taught her always to go to the inner booths first, leaving the outer booths for last in case a rush came in. Shelly saw the family needed shampoo and would soon run out of dishwashing detergent, so she got in line for the soaps booth.

Food-Mart's grocery division was composed of three dozen large booths, each set with a particular type of inventory. The booths, which consisted of deep, open-backed shelves and bins from which the associates could pull the requested items, were each manned by four to six cashiers. On the other side of the open shelves were shack-sized warehouses, where stock associates would keep a steady line of products coming as quickly as the cashier associates could pull them. The cashier associates wore bright red polo shirts with the words "Food-Mart" printed above their nametags, and khaki pants. The booths each stood at roughly the same size. The uniformity within the massive room was almost dizzying, almost like standing in the center of a very crowded house of mirrors. Shelley found that it brought out the claustrophobe in her.

"Attention, Food-Mart customers: a news associate in Area Three will be beginning broadcast in five minutes," the voice on the intercom reported, and then happily added: "Don't forget the face-masks when you stop by our health and beauty booth. Two-packs are on sale right now for only ten ninety-nine. Thank you for being a Food-Mart shopper!"

The lines moved slowly, but eventually Shelley made it to a register.

The cashier associate was young, probably just eighteen, and she had a smug look on her face. Shelley figured she would be smug, too, if being a Cashier for Food-Mart was the best she could ever do. Shelley felt thankful to have the opportunity to be more than a Mart employee, and then it struck her that her mother's income was what made it possible for both her and her brother to receive their requisite educations.

"What can I get you?" the cashier associate asked.

Shelley double-checked her list and then cleared her throat, afraid that her voice might crack when she spoke. She had never done the actual ordering before. In some strange, egocentric way, she felt on the spot. "Um, I need one dish soap and a large shampoo, please."

"Moisturizing or tearless?" the cashier associate asked.

Shelley looked back at the shelves and realized

that she had a small selection from which to choose. "Oh . . . moisturizing."

The associate plucked the two items from their shelves and brought them to her register. Both items had the same grey packaging with the word "Quality" stretched across the top at an angle. The moisturizing shampoo had a picture of a smiling woman sporting a shampoo hair-do. The dish soap had a picture of white dishes and lemon slices. The associate rang up both items using a scanning gun.

Shelley slid George's card through a machine then offered the associate one of her grocery bags. Pleased that she had finished her first transaction, she looked for the battery booth. Kurt had been abusing the bathroom click-light for weeks. He threw tantrums when anyone would try to turn it off, and he became hysterical when the light began to grow dimmer by the hour. He began waking in fearful, crying fits, and as much as Shelley loved her little brother, she was just about ready to lose her mind. Batteries were expensive, but right now, they were necessary for everyone's sake.

The battery line was much shorter than the soap line, but it moved slowly. Shelley saw that they were short a couple of cashier associates, and a manager was busy arguing with a customer over a denied refund. The customer refused to walk away, and the cashier associate standing before him stared quietly with her jaw agape.

Shelley took another deep breath, still struggling to abate her anxiety. Through the corner of her eye, she saw a woman who looked remarkably like Virginia. She turned with a gasp, only to realize her mind had played a cruel trick on her. No one among the crowd looked even remotely like her. She jumped as the loud speaker clicked on.

"Attention, Food-Mart customers: for the next thirty minutes the plastics booth will be discounting all recyclable food containers by ten percent," the voice announced. "And remember, it's the team player who ultimately gets ahead. Food-Mart values your customer loyalty."

Shelley turned and saw Charlotte standing in the cereal line with her mother. Both were wearing what appeared to be designer surgical facemasks, imprinted with pretty designs and a brand logo. Relieved to see her friend, Shelley waved.

Charlotte skipped over to her. "Hey, I thought that was you!"

Shelley nodded, unsure what to say.

"I haven't seen you around, but I heard what happened," Charlotte said. "I'm so sorry."

"Thanks."

The irate customer stormed off and the line began to move a little.

Charlotte's mother called to her, and she turned away for a moment to take a quick glance. "I gotta go. Sorry about . . . everything." She hurried off.

The line moved forward a little more, and Shelley moved a few paces toward the booth. When she finally got to the front of the line, she was met by another smug associate. She frowned as she noticed the batteries were each sold separately. The bathroom light only used one AA at a time, but Shelley knew Kurt would go through them quickly. She thought to buy several, but reconsidered when she saw that they were almost fifteen dollars each. It was no wonder her parents had always been so stingy about that light. "I'll take two AA," she said.

"That's it?" the associate asked.

Shelley nodded. She finished the transaction, putting the batteries in the same bag as the soaps.

"Attention, Food-Mart customers: a news associate in Area Three will be beginning broadcast in less than one minute," the loud speaker voice said. "Don't forget to buy this week's featured item: Quality freeze-dried mashed potato product, a family favorite, on sale all this week for only seven fifty-nine (limit three sale items, total). Thank you for shopping at Food-Mart."

Shelley stopped as she found the news associate over by the canned vegetables booth. There was already a small crowd gathering around him, and Shelley had to push past a few people to get a decent spot. A cashier associate quietly approached her with a wireless scan gun, and she held out her father's debit card for the associate to scan. The short man, who stood on a small platform holding an uncanny resemblance to a soapbox, had just started spouting the tidings for the day.

Shelley listened intently as the associate worked his way from the weather to the more important news: "Another wave of solar panel thefts has swept through the quadroplex, with Districts 89174 and 89148 being hit the hardest. This will be the third series of thefts like it this month. No suspects have been identified, but authorities believe that organized crime is likely to blame. Any questions?" He looked through the crowd. A young woman raised her hand,

and he pointed to her.

"Do authorities have any idea what thieves would want with solar panels?" the woman asked.

"They do not," the news associate answered. He glanced up and looked around for a moment in thought, then looked back at the woman. "Some say they might be finding a way to sell them through the black market, though."

There was a small clatter through the crowd as people nodded and murmured to one another over the associate's assessment.

No one else raised their hand, so the news associate continued: "A man was arrested for attempting to bribe his wife's doctor for antibiotics yesterday. His wife, who suffered from Lyme disease, killed herself earlier this morning." He paused for a moment, as if offering the woman a moment for her passing. "Any questions?" he finally asked. He panned the audience with his eyes, searching for hands.

"A deadly virus has killed dozens of residents throughout the quadroplex in just the past two weeks," the news associate continued. "Believed to be a biological weapon in powder form, authorities don't know who is behind its making, but they do know that a deviant terrorist group is randomly infecting humans. Concerned citizens should wear a facemask and plastic gloves while out in public. Any questions?"

Another young woman shot her arm into the air, and the news associate immediately pointed to her.

"What makes authorities suspect deviants?" the woman asked.

"That information is still undisclosed, but Corporate is advising that people avoid second-hand items and protect themselves while out in public," the news associate replied.

Shelley raised her hand. Her heart sped up as the news associate pointed and the crowd stared at her. She took a deep breath. "If deviants are responsible, does anyone know how they got a hold of a biological weapon?" she asked.

"Well. . . ." The news associate took a quick glance over the crowd, and Shelley turned to see if perhaps he was looking over at a teleprompter. Strangely, he seemed to be looking at nothing. She wondered what was over there that he could see and no one else could.

"Police-Corp has a few leads, but they're not disclosing any of them at this time," the associate finally said.

A young man had his hand raised, and the associate pointed to him.

"Can the virus be transferred between people?" he asked.

"They think not, but if you know someone who is sick, make sure you take precautions just in case." The news associate looked over the crowd for more hands before he continued on to tell them about the ever-rising price of electricity, a possible vegetable shortage by the end of the season, and a building collapse in District 89147, causing numerous injuries and substantial property damage.

It took Shelley over two hours to purchase the rest of the items on her list, and her hands were full by the time she got onto the shuttle back to Housing. The rain picked up, but luckily, transportation services continued to move. Shelley's bags grew heavier the longer she held them, but she dared not set them down in fear of someone else quickly claiming them. Luckily, the Line 250 shuttle gave her a direct shot back to Housing and she had only a short walk from the garage. She removed and discarded her mask and gloves as she entered the building.

As she approached her apartment, she noticed that William and Judith stood in the hallway, talking to George. William and Judith were both wearing facemasks and gloves, obviously assuming George was contagious. They had apparently given him a bottle of tequila, and he held the ribbon-decorated bottle close to his body with a protective grip. The group saw Shelley and moved so she could get all of her bags through the door. Tired and cranky, she dropped the bags just past the kitchen door and sat down beside the wall heater.

"Would you like to come in and help me drink this?" George asked William and Judith through the door, scratching at the week-old stubble on his face.

The couple exchanged glances, and then William very politely answered, "No."

"I'm sure you understand," Judith added. "You can't be too careful right now, and with the infection that took Virginia. . . ." Her voice trailed off, and she looked down.

William chimed back in, "We wish you the best. We really do."

George nodded. "Well, thanks for the tequila."

"Come by if there's anything you need," Judith said.

George smiled gratefully. "Will do."

William shrugged as the couple moved to their side of the hall. "What are neighbors for, right?" William opened the door, and they rushed inside, looking terrified that the virus might seek them out if they lingered in the hall any longer.

George closed and locked the door, and then took the bottle of tequila into the kitchen. He pulled a tumbler from the cupboard, poured himself a generous serving of the potent, amber liquid, and then sat down at the table. He took a swig of the drink, coughing lightly as it burned its way down to his stomach.

Shelley watched, curious. "It can't taste that bad."

"Well, you're not going to find out tonight, so don't ask." George took another swig, swallowing hard.

"I wasn't going to," Shelley lied. She got up and began putting away the groceries.

George looked terrible. He hadn't slept since he got the news about Virginia, and his hygiene had diminished considerably over the week.

Kurt stormed in. "Took you long enough! I'm starving! When's dinner?"

"I'm going to start it as soon as I'm done putting away the groceries," Shelley said.

"Are we going to have dinner in the dark again?" Kurt's voice rose an octave, the shrill whine pushing Shelley's patience.

She reminded herself that the boy was every bit as scared and confused as she was, so she forced a calm and patient "Maybe."

Kurt stomped his foot. "It's not fair!"

"Go play in your room, Kurt," George said.

"It's getting dark in my room!" Kurt cried.

"Then bring your toys in here. Dinner will be ready in a little while." He grimaced as he swallowed another shot of tequila.

Kurt gave George an angry scowl, but he didn't move.

Shelley dug the batteries out of one of the bags. "Kurt, look what I got for the click-light." She tossed one to him, and he caught it with both hands. "Why don't you change it out while we still have the kitchen light on?"

Kurt left with the battery, his pouty attitude somewhat diffused.

George poured himself another serving of tequila. He noticed that Shelley left out a package of spaghetti and canned sauce. Virginia always made spaghetti on Wednesdays.

Shelley put a pot of water on the stove to boil, then took her school bag to the kitchen table. She had a couple hours of homework still to do, and it would soon be time to turn off the kitchen light. She had the light in the bathroom if she really needed to get her work finished, but at this point, she wasn't sure she had the energy left even to get started. She took a look at her assignments with an overwhelmed sigh, unsure where to start.

## Chapter Ten

**"I** can't remember a thing," George said, his mind a blur and his thoughts confused. He sat in a small room, wearing a Police-Corp-issued jumpsuit. He winced at the pain that drummed in his head as he strained to search his memory. He remembered the earlier part of the night, but not much of it. He had sent both of the kids to bed early, intent on getting as drunk as he possibly could. Beyond that, the details were sketchy.

To accommodate Kurt's escalating anxiety attacks, Shelley had begun to sleep on the floor in his room. She made up a new bedtime story for him each night, talking until he fell asleep so that he knew, despite the dark, that she was still in there with him. George remembered listening in on Shelley's tale for the night, caught up just as deeply as Kurt was in her attention to detail and flair with words.

He had abandoned the tumbler after several servings, opting to drink directly from the bottle instead. He had been drunk before, so he knew what hell might find him when morning came, but for the moment he reveled in the numb bliss each swallow promised to bring closer.

Still listening to Shelley's story, George moved to his bedroom. He took another swig from the bottle before setting it down on the nightstand. He moved to Virginia's pillow and brought it up to his face. He breathed deeply, searching for any remains of the scent that had once been there. He breathed deeper, but still he couldn't find any trace of it. She was gone.

George's throat knotted as he contemplated the emptiness slowly consuming him. He choked and coughed as he forced down another huge swig of tequila. Then, all of a sudden, he began to have difficulty sitting upright. He was only able to get to the side of the bed before he began to vomit.

He remembered staggering to the bathroom, leaning against the wall to keep from falling over. He rinsed his face and drank some water, lowering to the floor as he felt the onset of more nausea. He closed his eyes and the darkness immediately seized him.

The next thing he knew, he was coming to in a holding cell.

He squinted, the overhead light stinging his eyes. He looked back and forth between the two police associates, both large men with unforgiving faces. He rubbed his tired eyes, trying to conceal the fact that they were beginning to well up. "Listen. My wife died. I got drunk and blacked out. I don't know what else to tell you."

"You don't remember anything else?" the associate on George's left asked.

George searched the deepest regions of his mind, but last night continued to come back as a blank, black slate. He shook his head. "I have no idea. Will you just tell me what I'm in here for? And where are my kids?"

"They're fine. They're being held downstairs in the Safe House. Cooperate with us, and we'll get you to them as soon as possible."

The second associate pulled a digital camera from his bag and plugged it into a console at his side. A hologram popped up from the center of the table, displaying a three-dimensional image of a living room in disarray. George did not recognize it.

"This is a picture taken from your neighbor's apartment across the hall. You know William and Judith Rockwell, don't you?" the associate asked.

"I know them," George said, unsure what to make of the picture.

"You don't remember pounding on their door at three a.m., and then forcing your way in when Mr. Rockwell answered?" the associate continued.

George shook his head just as a flash of recollection hit him. In his drunken stupor, he had decided he needed a shoulder to cry on. When William had turned him away and Judith threatened to call Police-Corp when he refused to back out of the doorway, he had become enraged with his neighbors' seeming apathy.

George looked up at the associate with a surprised face. "I picked a fight with William. Oh, God . . . is he okay?"

"He's fine, but there was substantial damage sustained throughout his apartment. Housing is charging you eight thousand dollars for all of the wall and furnishing repairs, and we're still waiting to see if anyone is going to press additional charges," the associate on the right said as he went through his notes.

"Substantial damage?" George asked.

The associate on the left pushed a button on his camera and the hologram shifted to a close up of some of the damage. A broken chair sat over a shattered mirror, and there were several holes in the walls.

George stared at the picture in disbelief. "I did that?"

The associate unplugged the camera, and the holographic image instantly disappeared. "As it stands, you're being charged with disorderly conduct outside your home, damage to corporate property, and resisting arrest. Would you like a defense associate from Law-Corp to defend your case?"

"No," George said. With his luck, William would be the one who ended up the case's supervising manager. He looked down, breathing heavily. "I plead guilty to the charge."

The two police associates looked at one another, and then the one on the right stood. "Sit tight. I'll be back in a few minutes." The associate slipped out, leaving his partner alone with George.

George looked up, and he and the remaining associate stared one another down for a moment. George couldn't fight the impulse to look away, and he pretended to study the computer console on the side of the desk. He glanced back over at the associate, finding the man still staring at him, and he quickly looked down. To avoid looking back up, he traced the faux wood grain lines on the desk with his eyes.

"I don't know what I'd do if my wife died," the police associate said, his voice low and sympathetic.

George looked up, surprised. "She was a good woman. She didn't deserve what happened."

The associate nodded, his face remaining hard and cold. "My condolences to you."

George gave an abrupt, grateful nod.

Both men turned as the other associate entered with a small handheld computer. The top screen contained George's confession in twelve-point Courier. Below the smaller bottom screen, a plastic stylus sat in a fitted groove, and the associate plucked it out and handed to George.

George read the statement to ensure it was correct, and then signed his name in the bottom screen. A pixilated version of his signature came up on the screen as he signed. He looked it over one last time, and then snapped the stylus back into its receptacle and returned it to the associate.

"It shouldn't be too long until we know whether or not we can release you," the associate said as he saved George's signature into a database and turned off the computer. "You're going to have to return to the holding cell in the meantime."

The other associate stood as his partner handcuffed George, and the three moved together back toward the holding cells. The long hallway was obscenely bright, bringing George's headache to a new level of pain. He leaned over and began to heave.

The police associates dragged him on, unfazed. They entered an electronically secure corridor that contained five large holding cells. The associates put

George back into the drunk tank, the only cell not crowded with deviants and violent criminals.

The room had three gray walls, with a row of bars along the front in place of the fourth, and despite the circulation between it and the corridor, it reeked of vomit and urine. One other middle-aged man was in there, lying on his side, half-awake. He wore a Furniture-Mart associate polo shirt and khaki pants. He had thrown up on himself while passed out, but he was not yet awake enough to acknowledge the smelly mess that lingered on his face and in his hair.

George sat down as the police associates locked the door and walked off. He heard one of the associates call out a number, but he yawned as the man spoke and he didn't hear it. His number had already been called, his ticket taken; there was no need to pay attention now. He heard a door down the corridor open and then slam back shut as the associates escorted another prisoner into the interrogation room.

The other man in George's cell slowly came to, wiping the crusty hair from his face. He sat up, realizing he was not alone, and he gave George a hard scowl.

George turned away from the man. He was in no mood for another altercation. His head still pounded, but at least the nausea had subsided. He slouched back in his chair and closed his eyes, hoping he might sleep through his remaining hours of confinement. George knew Law-Corp, and when it all came down to it, humans were rarely incarcerated anymore. Deviants filled the majority of the prisons, amongst the occasional human murderer or rapist. It would take no more than a couple more hours for management to process his paperwork, and then he and the kids would be free to return home. He wasn't sure how he was going to pay Housing for the damage he'd done to the Rockwells' living room, but he would worry about it after he ensured that what remained of his family was safe at home.

He had no idea how to track the hours, as the cell had no windows, there were no visible clocks, and the associates had taken his watch. He dozed for a short time, waking to find the other man trying to remove his shoes. He kicked the man away, securing his shoes with the retying of both laces, keeping one eye on the man to make sure he didn't come tearing back in some crazed, hung-over rage. He looked up as the man decided to return to his cot, a mix of anger and guilt complicating his face.

George decided that the man was no real threat, but he stared him down for a moment just to establish that he was not to be assaulted again.

The other man looked down, ashamed to have been caught in the act. "I'm sorry, sir," he said going by work status rather than age to determine their hierarchy, knowing by George's nice shoes that he was a member of the Corp Segregate.

"Just stay on your side of the cell," George said in his most authoritative voice.

"I just thought that . . . I've been arrested for getting drunk a few times now, I thought they might go easy on me if I was wearing nicer shoes. What was your number, by the way?" He pulled a ticket from his pocket, making sure it was still there. On the ticket was a series of numbers, followed by the number sixty-three in bold lettering.

George shrugged. "I don't remember. Sorry."

The man looked up, and then a glimmer of recognition lit up his face. "George?"

George studied the man's face, unable to place it. "I'm sorry . . . do I know you?"

The man stood. "Edgar Lowe, from District 89147."

George sat up at the edge of his seat, his face suddenly bringing to mind images of a dark haired little boy. "Edgar?" He and Edgar had been good friends in grade school, before George's family had moved underground and the segregates had become fully defined. The boys had used to play by the creek, catching frogs and various flying bugs. The heavy rains eventually flooded over the river and turned the area into a disease-infested marshland. "Go figure," George said, breathing a nostalgic sigh.

Back when George and Edgar were friends, adults were still allowed to drive fuel-efficient cars, public schools all taught the same curriculum, and deviants still had equal rights. People were more relaxed, and the world seemed to have just a little more color to it. The weather could still be forecasted, even if it was already changing all over the globe.

George gave Edgar a weak smile. "How have you been?"

Edgar shrugged. "I think Police-Corp owns about half of my assets, and I'm about to be charged with a third offense, but other than that, life has been good and boring."

George nodded, not wanting to know any further details. He felt bad, but Edgar just didn't belong to his social group. Mart employees worked where they did because of their intelligence level and social standing. Like deviants, many of them didn't go to church or even pay their tithing. They wore their clothes several times before washing them, and most couldn't afford to clean their water recyclers more than once or twice a year. As a result, they often smelled less than desirable. George wondered if he was in any danger of catching some type of louse.

"I work for Law-Corp," George said, hoping Edgar might get the hint.

"You and your wife should come over for dinner sometime," Edgar said with a smile, misconstruing George's message to be nothing more than a pretentious boast. "My wife makes the most amazing no-cook faux apple pie."

George looked down. "My wife just died."

"Oh . . . I'm sorry."

George didn't respond. He moved to the bars as two officers appeared from the far end of the corridor. "Number sixty-three," one of them called.

Edgar perked up as if he had just won a raffle. "Right here!"

The officers unlocked the cell and escorted him away.

"Excuse me!" George called after them. "Is there any way anyone could check up on my case? George Irwin? I should have been processed by now, I think, and—"

"We'll look into it," one of the officers yelled back right before they disappeared into the brightly lit hall.

George began to pace, feeling impatient. He was glad to have the entire cell to himself, although

Edgar's absence did nothing for the nauseating smell of the place. After only a few minutes, George returned to the bars and looked as far as he could down the corridor. "Hello?" he called.

"What the hell are you trying to do?" hissed a young deviant in the cell across the way. "If you agitate them, they'll only keep you here longer!"

"And you know this from personal experience?" George asked.

The deviant shrugged. "Whatever, man. Scream like an idiot and see where it gets you. We all could use the entertainment."

A few others snickered as George retreated to the back of the cell, face flushed, and he returned to his seat without another word. He knew there was a process that every case had to go through, and paperwork could only be pushed so fast through the many desks it had to clear. He wondered what his file looked like. There were likely statements from both William and Judith, as well as from any of the neighbors who might possibly have seen or heard something worth mentioning. There would be a printout of the pictures he was shown as well as his signed confession. He wondered what his computer questionnaire would look like, and he pictured it in his mind's eye:

*Did the Defendant confess to his/her crime(s)? (Research associate #02007-841 said "Yes.") Click HERE to agree. Click HERE to disagree.*

*Does the paperwork indicate that the Defendant showed remorse for said crime(s)?*
*(Research associate #02007-841 said "Yes.")*
*Click HERE to agree.*
*Click HERE to disagree.*

*Does the paperwork indicate that the Defendant could have made a profit by committing said crime(s)?*
*(Research associate #00453-584 said "No.")*
*Click HERE to agree.*
*Click HERE to disagree.*

*Has the Defendant ever been convicted of any previous crimes?*
*(Research associate #01002-388 said "No.")*
*Click HERE to agree.*
*Click HERE to disagree.*

*Does the Defendant have anything to say in his/her defense, for having committed said crime(s)?*
*(Research associate #02007-841 said "No.")*
*Click HERE to agree.*
*Click HERE to disagree.*

George knew his confession would ensure a guilty verdict, but also that his cooperation with the police associates would help to make it more likely that his fine didn't eat up too much of his monthly income. The fact that his wife had just died, and that all of his actions occurred during a blackout, would be included in his report. Hopefully, no one with the means and desire to destroy George would end up with it moving across his desk.

He stood as a police manager stopped at George's cell.

"George Irwin?" the manager asked.

"That's me."

The manager's eyes shifted uncomfortably, and he cleared his throat before he spoke: "I'm sorry, but it seems your file has been misplaced, and we can't release you until it turns up. If the managers at Law-Corp can't process it by dusk, you're going to have to stay the night."

"What?" George felt as if a hot blast of wind were forcing him back, and he found the nearest seat. "Please tell me you're joking." He began to sweat, and he wiped his face with his shirtsleeve.

"I'm afraid I'm not," the manager said. "If you'd like to speak to my supervisor about it, I'm sure I can find him."

"What about my kids?" George asked, closing his eyes, his body feeling hot and fluid.

"Well, unless you have a relative in the district we can release them to, they'll just have to stay the night at the Safe House."

George strained to glance back over at the police manager. He shook his head then looked down. "I'm a manager for Law-Corp. How come I've never heard of anything like this happening before?"

The police manager shrugged. "I'll be sure to ask my supervisor when I see him." He walked off, ignoring George's pleas to return.

# Chapter Eleven

Virginia rinsed her hair one last time, hoping the timer on the water recycler would not go off before she could get all of the soap out. She grabbed her towel and made way for another woman who stood, naked and shaking, waiting for her turn. There was a clean pair of hospital pajamas waiting for her on her bed, and she quickly got dressed with her body turned away from the rest of the room. The weekly ordeal they made of bathing the group was humiliating.

Virginia wrapped her hair in her towel, glad at least to have had a shower. The nozzles only worked when the medical associates turned them on, and the once a week that they did turn them on was just not often enough. By then, not one person was without a hefty odor and slick, oily hair. Virginia splashed herself off using the sink water when she got the chance, but cold water and powdered hand soap did little to keep the filth at bay. It was mortifying to be herded into the bathroom by the medical associates in such a way, but it was over with for now and at least for the moment she was clean.

Emily took her time walking over to Virginia, shaking the towel over her wet hair and adjusting the fit of her pajamas. Both of them turned around and faced the far wall as the associates instructed the men to remove their clothes and line up for their shower.

"When we get out of here, I will never take my privacy for granted ever again," Emily said, resting her towel over her shoulders. "I bet this is how they treat prison inmates."

Virginia nodded grimly. "At least the ones who happen to have the wrong eye color."

Emily nodded her agreement. Her face went painfully sober as she suddenly questioned aloud, "I wonder if I'll still be able to work as a cashier associate at my booth? Deviants don't work as cashier associates."

Virginia suddenly had to apply the same question to her own job. Had so much changed about her that she was now no longer qualified to handle one of Communications-Corp's switchboards? She and Emily looked at one another as the same question hit them both at once: Would they be able to convince anyone, including their loved ones, that absolutely nothing about them had changed other than their eye color?

"My fiancé hates deviants!" Emily said, the reality of their situation finally sinking in. "My life is ruined!"

"My husband isn't too fond of them, either," Virginia said, denial forcing her to add, "I know he loves me, though, and I know my kids love me. I know that won't change."

Emily began to cry.

"Don't cry, sweetie," Virginia said, her throat knotting up. "Everything will be okay. You'll see."

Emily shook her head. "No. I don't think it will." She stood and turned.

Virginia reached for Emily's shoulder, but she brushed her aside. She watched as Emily walked in long strides, almost in slow motion, toward the medical associates standing in front of the bathroom door. Virginia wanted to get up and run after her, but she felt frozen where she sat, knowing deep down that there was nothing she could do. She watched helplessly as Emily signed her life away.

Emily turned back as she passed through the door, her eyes haunting as she gave Virginia one last pained smile. She crossed the threshold and the door closed behind her.

And then she was gone.

Virginia grieved silently as Olaf, a friendly older man, exited the bathroom and got dressed.

He hurried up to her, his hair and beard still dripping. "Where's Emily?"

Virginia looked down. "She left."

Olaf sat down, his body flushing. "Where did she go?"

Virginia turned back to him, the tears streaming from her eyes speaking louder than any words she might have to offer him.

"But why?" Olaf asked, his eyes welling up. "She was so young! She had her whole life ahead of her!"

Virginia shook her head, wishing that she had tried harder to hold Emily back. "I couldn't stop her," she said, trying to amend the memory of it in her mind.

"Damn it all!" Olaf cried, going to his bed and lying down.

Virginia surveyed the room, unsure how much longer she would be able to handle being there herself. There were now exactly four men and four women left, including her. She wondered if the medical management was simply counting on the group to give up, one by one, until no one remained. Perhaps those who persisted were doing nothing but prolonging the inevitable.

Virginia watched the camera sweep back and forth, flipping it off once as it passed over her.

The showers turned off and the medical associates left the room. The locks clicked shut. The last of the men dried off and got dressed. No one else seemed to care that Emily had given up. Few even seemed to notice that she was gone.

The locks clicked back open, and one of the medical associates who had just overseen the showers returned with the manager and two security associates. He had an order from Corporate, just downloaded onto his handheld computer.

"After due consideration, Corporate has decided to give you two options." The medical associate cleared his throat, glancing down at his computer screen. He punched in a code, bringing up the downloaded file. "Corporate is interested in a study on live subjects infected with what we have named retrovirus HD-1, to study your antibodies and develop a vaccine. All those not interested in participating in the study will be euthanized."

Virginia and Olaf glanced over at one another in disbelief.

The medical manager stepped forward. "We'll need your signatures on the appropriate forms, so if you could all come forward in an orderly manner."

Olaf winked at Virginia, then suddenly sprang out of bed and grabbed the man in the next bed over. He yanked the man to the ground and put him in a stranglehold, and then braced himself for the security associates' attack. "I'll see you all in Hell!"

Olaf's attack put the entire room into a panic, and the medical associate ran into the center of the room in an attempt to back up Security. The medical manager tackled a woman who ran ahead of Virginia in an attempt to escape, and by the time he turned to secure the door, Virginia and three others had already scattered.

The medical manager slipped out the door and locked it, making a mental note to let out his personnel as soon as the building was secure. "Security breach!" he yelled, running after a young man who was unfortunate enough to have slipped out last. The manager stopped at an emergency alarm station, catching his breath as he sounded the alarm.

"I need backup here!" the manager yelled as he chased the young man to a dead end. He tackled the young man, knocking him off his feet, and all nearby personnel moved to assist in his capture.

Virginia slipped unseen into an unlocked utility closet. The small room had a washer and dryer, bins of dirty laundry, and cleaning supplies arranged on open shelves. Knowing the search for her would be thorough, she considered her hiding places. If she simply knelt behind the dryer she was sure to be found, and the same likely went for hiding inside the hot machine. She hurried to the vent to the central heating duct, but found it tightly secured. She snatched a putty knife from a nearby shelf and used it to pry off the screen, then carefully slid off the vent and slipped inside the tight area, slamming the vent back into place behind her.

Virginia quietly wriggled back a few feet, then froze as she heard the closet door open. She heard the security associate step through the room. The man checked the washer and dryer, and then poked through the piles of laundry. Virginia held her breath and closed her eyes as he peered through the vent, straining to see as far into the shadows as he could. After only a moment, the associate moved away from the vent and left the room. Virginia took a deep breath as the door shut behind him. She waited a few minutes to ensure he hadn't left just to get reinforcements, and then she worked her way back up to the vent.

She looked around the room, trying to determine whether she had any chance at escape. There didn't seem like any way out. She could dig through the dirty linen on the chance that there was a pair of scrubs hidden in the bin, but she didn't think that would be very likely. Even if she did find some type of medical associate uniform, her eye color would give her away before she could get down the hall.

She slid back as the door opened again, and she could just see into the closet as a sanitation worker came in with a rolling mop bucket.

The skinny young woman pushed the bucket into a corner and began a load of laundry with a groan. The washing machine was loud as it filled with hot water, the sound echoing through the narrow duct.

Virginia slid back up to the vent, getting a better look, and she realized that the sanitation associate was a deviant. Without another thought, in one quick motion, Virginia knocked out the vent and slid out of the duct. She slammed into the surprised young woman, pinning her against the far wall and covering her mouth.

"I need your help!" Virginia cried.

The sanitation associate nodded, and Virginia slowly let her go.

"You have to get me out of here!" Virginia continued. "I'm being held against my will!"

"You're one of the virus victims?"

Virginia hadn't expected such a question to come from a sanitation associate, and she gave the deviant a suspicious eye. "How did you know?"

The young woman moved to a bin of clean sheets, picking up as much of the unfolded pile as she could hold. "Get in."

Virginia got into the bin, and the young associate dropped the pile of sheets over her. "Sit tight." The young woman dug into her pockets, pulling out syringes, test tubes, and a few other objects she had stolen from the medical offices, and stuffed them under the pile. She finished loading the washing machine and then deftly rolled Virginia and her laboratory supplies out of the closet.

She rolled the heavy bin to a service elevator and quietly accompanied the load down to the basement. She rolled the bin to the folding piles at the end of the corridor and lugged the laundry off Virginia.

"Thank you so much!" Virginia said, climbing out

of the bin.

"It's the least I can do," the deviant said. She extended her hand. "I'm Anne."

"Virginia."

They shook.

"Do you have anywhere to go?" Anne asked, checking to make sure that no one else was in the vicinity.

"I plan on going home."

"Do you think that's wise?" Anne collected the laboratory supplies, wrapped them in a pajama top she snagged from a laundry pile, and then stashed them behind a trash bin.

Virginia shrugged. "Where else would I go?"

Anne found a piece of scratch paper and a pen, and wrote down shuttle and walking directions to a remote location. She handed it to Virginia with a smile. "Ask for Ray." She shoved Virginia behind a pile of laundry and tried to look busy as a sanitation manager crossed the far corridor and then disappeared around another corner.

Virginia took the piece of paper. "How do I get out of here?"

After a moment of thought, Anne quickly wriggled out of her uniform and tossed it to Virginia. She kicked off her shoes. "I'm not sure it'll be a perfect fit, but it's all I've got." She began to dig through a utility drawer until she came across a roll of duct tape.

Virginia squeezed herself into Anne's uniform and forced her feet into the tiny shoes.

Anne tossed Virginia the duct tape and her shuttle pass, then crossed her wrists behind her back. "I can't look like a willing participant in this."

Virginia bound Anne's wrists behind her back and wrapped the tape around her ankles.

Anne dropped onto a pile of clean pajama tops. "The parking garage is down the hall to your left, and then up one floor. Now, tape up my mouth and get out of here."

"Tape your mouth?"

Anne gave a frustrated huff. "You want to make it look authentic, right?"

"Are you sure someone will find you?"

"Positive." Anne glanced down to the end of the hall, looking nervous. "Will you stop wasting time?"

Virginia reluctantly slapped a piece of tape over Anne's mouth. "Thanks again." She hurried down the long hallway, pocketing Anne's shuttle directions as she took the stairwell up to the garage. She found a direct shuttle line to Housing.

She took a long, deep breath as the shuttle rolled away from the platform. She wondered if any of the others who had escaped were also able to get away, hoping she wasn't the only one. She wondered how many more people would find themselves in her situation before Medical-Corp was able to come up with a vaccine or antidote, if either was even possible.

Virginia couldn't reach Housing quickly enough, and she gazed through the window at the heavy rain as the shuttle lurched along its track. It was dark and grey out, and heavy clouds blocked out the early evening sky.

She knocked on her front door, nervous but excited. She assumed George and the kids would be home, given the time, and her heart sank when she knocked several times and no one came to the door.

"Hello?" Virginia knocked again. "It's me!"

The door cracked open across the way, and Judith peeked out. Virginia turned, and Judith quickly shut the door as she noticed Virginia's deviant eyes. Virginia stood in the center of the hallway, unsure what to do. She decided to knock on the Rockwells' door just as William opened it, Judith huddling behind him.

"I don't have my key," Virginia said.

"You're dead!" William said. He couldn't stop looking at her eyes.

"They lied!" Virginia began to cry, more due to panic than the despair also seizing her.

Judith remained behind the safety of her husband, eyeing Virginia suspiciously. "I think we should call for a security associate!"

"It *looks* like Virginia," William said.

"Where is my family?" Virginia cried. "I just want to see my family!"

"They've been gone for a couple of days," William said.

"What do you think you're doing?" Judith slapped William on the shoulder, and she slammed the door shut.

Her gut telling her that security associates would soon be on their way to clear the floor, Virginia hurried to the stairwell. She passed a young woman slowly helping her young daughter up the stairs.

The little girl looked over Virginia and smiled. "Mommy! Look at her pretty eyes!"

The woman scowled at Virginia, yanking the girl up into her arms. "We don't talk to deviants, Angie," the woman scolded, and then the two disappeared through the door to the second floor.

Virginia hurried out of the building, running down the halls toward the shuttle garage. She dug out Anne's directions from her pocket. The shuttle changes led to an area where Virginia had never been before, but she wasn't sure if she really had anywhere else to go. Using Anne's pass, Virginia boarded the Line 270 shuttle, sat down, and closed her eyes.

# Chapter Twelve

If Corporate had any idea where George's file had been misplaced, its managers had taken their time tracking it down. By the time George had his release process work ready to sign, he found himself cheated out of another entire day. That the managers rushed to get his processing finished now was of little meaning. He'd been forced to miss two days of work, but he would have to wait until Monday to find out if he still had a job.

He now owed Police-Corp close to twenty thousand in fines, on top of what he owed Housing for the Rockwells' broken window. If he defaulted on his payments, even once, there would be a warrant for his arrest and he would ultimately end up owing the system even more. George had a difficult time covering the family's expenses as it was, and there was no question that either Shelley or Kurt would have to be moved back into the Mart Education System on their current budget. The knowledge that he had to make this choice, and immediately, made him feel like hope truly had left his world for good.

Leigh M. Lane

One of his children would be doomed to a life of impoverished monotony, and there was nothing he could do about it.

He weighed the potential in each of them as he took the stairs down to the Safe House. Based on their grades, they both had the intelligence to work middle management. He had already invested in Shelley for several years, Kurt having been in the Corp Education System for only three. Shelley's status as a woman would limit her positions, however, given Corporate America's views on family values. No doubt Shelley would be encouraged to marry early into her adulthood, and only to take a part-time job if she planned to have children. Kurt could take any job, no matter when he started his family. Moreover, unlike Shelley, he had dark brown eyes. The boy had more options.

George found the office he had been directed to, a dim room packed with rows of chairs and distraught, displaced people. He went up to the secretary associate. "I'm here for my two kids," he said through the Plexiglas security window.

The secretary associate pointed through the window, to a small computer anchored to the wall. "Fill out the form and have a seat."

George filled out the short form, identifying himself and his two children. He signed his name in the signature box, then found an empty chair as far away as he could possibly get from the rest of the sorry people in there.

From the looks of the room and all the people in it, George expected to wait at least an hour or so, and he was pleasantly surprised when Shelley and Kurt emerged from a back room only a few minutes later.

Kurt ran to George, coughing and sobbing between tearful fits, while Shelly sauntered over to him slowly and angrily. George picked up Kurt and offered Shelley a refused hug, and then the three left together and caught the shuttle back to Housing. The rain picked up and the shuttle moved slowly, threatening to stall every few yards. The three remained silent despite the ridiculously long ride, waiting to get home before discussing their confinement.

"How could you get arrested like that? Do you have any idea how boring the Safe House was?" Shelley began as they entered their cold, dark apartment. "It was hellish!"

"Try a jail cell for two days," George replied, turning on the kitchen light.

"It was like we were in kid-jail!" Kurt said, needing to be a part of the conversation.

Shelley went to the wall heater and turned it on, and the three huddled as close to the grill as they could without being burned.

"Are we having chicken nuggets for dinner tonight?" Kurt asked.

Shelley nodded, although her face looked tired and bitter. "Just let me warm up a minute."

The news about Shelley's education ate at George more and more the longer he sat with it. Telling Shelley would not be easy. He practiced in his mind what he would say to her, finding no way to buffer the actual blow. He turned to her, deciding that further procrastination would get him nowhere.

"I owe a lot of money because of what I did." He looked down, unwilling to see her face when he told her: "I can't afford to put you through Corp school any longer."

Shelley took a deep breath and moved to reply, but then sealed her lips and stormed across the kitchen. She pulled a package of pre-breaded chicken nuggets from the icebox and arranged them in a glass baking dish, unable to hide that she had begun to cry.

"I'm really sorry, sweetie," George said.

"So I'm supposed to go to Mart school?" she asked, not turning around. She put the chicken nuggets in the microwave and set the timer.

"Would you rather I move Kurt instead?"

"Move where?" Kurt asked, surprise and terror in his voice.

"Nowhere," George reassured him.

They all knew about the gang problems, the drugs, and the violence that occurred in the Mart Education System. Still, there was heavy tension over the unspoken question: Why had George chosen Kurt over her?

"When do I start?" she asked.

"I have to work out the change in payment arrangements tomorrow, so I'm assuming the switch will be immediate," George said with a sigh.

Shelley pulled a can of corn from the cupboard and emptied it into a shallow saucepan. She turned on the stove, placing the saucepan over the lone burner.

"I have to say, you're taking this really well," George said, feeling a little relieved.

"How did you expect me to take it?" Shelley asked, keeping her voice level and calm.

George shrugged. "I wasn't really sure, but I'm relieved that you understand."

"Dinner will be ready in just a minute," Shelley said, ignoring George's last comment. "Serve yourself." She hurried out of the kitchen in a dramatic display.

George served Kurt, wondering if he should follow Shelley. They had all already lost so much within the past few days, and he knew that this latest blow had to be devastating. George lost both of his parents to the tail-end of the tuberculosis epidemic. He had been working for Law-Corp for just a few years, and he had only just met Virginia. Because he was forced to move across the quadroplex, to District 89150, he never saw his parents after he moved, and he learned about their illness by telephone. When he got the news that they died, he held onto his sanity by losing himself in his job.

What did Shelley have left?

The bathroom door slammed shut.

"Daddy, why's Shelley so mad?"

"She's just sad, buddy."

Kurt nodded.

George gave Kurt a kiss on the forehead then went down the hall. He tried the bathroom door, finding it locked. "Shelley?"

"Go away!"

"Come on, now! I'm doing my best here! What am I supposed to do?"

"Not get drunk and ruin my life!" she cried.

He took a deep breath, then sat down beside the door and waited for her to say something more. She met him with only continued silence.

Finally, he decided to try again. "Shelley? I'm really sorry."

"Ha!"

"It was inevitable, anyway! We're living off a single income now. We've all got to make our sacrifices if we're going to get through this," he said. Another sad sigh escaped him as she refrained from any further response. He turned as Kurt met him in the hall.

"Why are you fighting?" Kurt asked.

George sat forward and put a reassuring hand on Kurt's shoulder. "Why don't you go in your room and play? Everything's fine."

Kurt crossed his arms, a subtle scowl giving him an angry, pouty face.

"Go play, buddy."

Kurt turned to the door. "Shelley, what's wrong?"

"I just need to cool off," Shelley said.

George got to his feet. "Okay. I've had enough of this." He reached over the door's upper threshold, pulling a key from atop the paneling. He nudged Kurt aside as he unlocked the door and threw it open.

Shelley scrambled to gather the pens and short stack of papers that lay before her.

George stormed in. "What is this? Where did you get these?"

"Please—just let me have this!" Shelley cried, holding her writing supplies close.

"Do you know what would happen if—"

"I don't care!" she cried. "I don't have any future, anyway, so why not do what I want to do?"

"Because you know that's not how it works, sweetie."

She turned away defensively. "I don't care how it works!"

Kurt began to cry. "Please stop fighting!"

Both turned to Kurt, falling silent.

He shifted his glance between the two of them, dumbfounded by their response. He sniffled, going quiet himself, waiting to see what either would do next.

"May I see?" George finally asked her, his voice light and inquisitive.

Slowly, her hand shaking, she offered him one of the pieces of thick, pulpy paper.

George carefully read the poem:

Sickly blue,
    pale windows to an empty shell,
    Pestilent and putrid;
    when will your luster die?

Twisted membrane,
    a matter of grey gone black,
    Rotten and deformed;
    when will your last spark fire?

Fraudulent body,
    true colors feigned with closed eyes,
    Foul and tainted;
    when will you go still?

George nodded. "I like it."

"You do?" Shelley asked, surprised.

"Why don't you come out and write by the heater, so we can turn out the click-light?"

She nodded, and the three returned together to the warming kitchen.

# Chapter Thirteen

The Line 270 shuttle inched itself toward the garage, finally approaching its destination after nearly a two-hour power delay. Had it not been thirty degrees out, raining and hailing in heavy waves, Virginia would have tried her luck finishing her way across the district on foot. She had enough tunnel and outdoor travel ahead of her with just the shuttle transfers as it stood, however, and as uncomfortably crowded as the shuttle was, at least it provided enough body heat inside to keep a person from freezing to death.

The Line 50 shuttle seemed to move faster. It also moved more deviants than humans, which filled Virginia with a strange mix of discomfort and ease. She could look around the shuttle without calling attention to herself, but at the same time, being surrounded by so many natural deviants at once elicited a programmed response from within her that she couldn't just rationalize away. She could feel heavy beads of sweat begin to trickle down her forehead and over the core of her body, and she started to shiver.

A young deviant woman, also dressed in a sanitation associate's uniform, turned to Virginia. "Are you okay?" she asked, sincere concern in her crystalline blue eyes.

Virginia nodded, although it was clear that she was beginning to panic. She felt herself go dizzy, and she closed her eyes for a moment in attempt to regain her composure.

"Try to slow down your breathing," the woman said, her voice calming.

Virginia nodded, although she struggled to catch her breath. She felt like she was suffocating no matter how hard she worked to control her heavy lungs.

The shuttle came to a stop in a smaller garage, and Virginia forced herself to her feet. Still feeling uneasy and dizzy with overwhelm, she exited the shuttle and looked for the Line 70 shuttle track.

The young woman came up beside Virginia, setting down her heavy backpack. "Are you lost?"

Virginia showed her Anne's directions. "I've never been on this side of town before."

"I gathered," she said. She helped Virginia to the correct bench, shouldering her backpack, and then sat down with her. "I'm Mary."

"Virginia."

They shook hands.

"I know where you're going. I can take you there," Mary said.

Virginia smiled gratefully, although she could not wipe the desperation that still riddled her thoughts. "That's very kind of you."

"I just happen to be on my way there, myself,"

Mary said. She patted her backpack. "I have a present from Power-Corp."

The Line 70 shuttle came in from the left, its brakes squealing as it slowed to a halt in front of them. The doors opened, and Virginia, Mary, and three other deviants were the only people to board. Strangely, the shuttle had no security associate.

"Who's your friend?" the only man on board asked Mary. He was young, had dark, shaggy hair, and wore paint-spattered overalls. His hands were covered with scars, and he carried a large bag. It looked heavy.

"This is Virginia," Mary began. "She's new to this area. Anne gave her directions from the hospital."

The young man nodded. He smiled and extended his hand to Virginia. "I'm Isaac."

Virginia shook his hand, surprised by his grip. "So you both know Anne?" she asked.

"We're all colleagues," Mary said.

"Colleagues?"

"Who *is* this woman?" Isaac asked, looking suspicious.

"A casualty of war," Mary replied, an answer that seemed to satisfy all but Virginia.

Virginia looked around the shuttle car, suddenly realizing that she was the only one there who was not in on the secret. "What war?"

"Ray will explain everything," Mary assured her.

No one said another word as the shuttle slowed, coming to a stop at a small, private hub rather than in a garage. The rain and hail both continued to come down relentlessly, and the passengers braced themselves as the door opened.

"This is our stop," Mary said.

All five deviants stepped out, immediately getting soaked by the cold rain. They shielded their heads and faces from the hail, and all of them began to run down a muddy path carved through a tall, thick field of wild grass.

Virginia had no idea what she was doing or where specifically she was going, but she ran along with the group, cold and shivering in the rain. Hailstones the size of marbles pummeled the group, and the wind was painfully cold. Visibility was low. The group moved through the trail as quickly as they could. Virginia felt a strange sense of excitement take over her. She felt herself delving far beyond her comfort zone, but at the same time, she was on an adventure to somewhere unknown. She knew she had to let go of everything that had made up her life as Virginia Irwin or she would go insane. She told herself that she needed to embrace whatever the future had for her. Corporate may have taken away her identity, but she was still alive.

Virginia felt her wedding band, wondering what place it had in her new life. The thought of discarding it was enough to return the lump to her throat, and so she moved it to her right hand instead. It felt funny there, foreign. It would take some getting used to, just as it had so many years ago when George first placed it on her finger and she swore her eternal vows. She wondered if George had moved his band yet, being just as much the false widower as she was the false widow.

She hoped he would not grieve too long for her.

The group came up to a parked shuttle at the end of a private line. It sat silent and dark.

"Thank goodness we don't have to wait today!" Mary said, pulling open the shuttle associate's door. She got in, and after only a moment the interior of the shuttle lit up and the main door slid open. Virginia followed the rest of the group into the shuttle, glad that she had more than just Anne's vague directions to get her to her destination. Anne had to have counted on her to stand out by the time she boarded the 70, she figured, because it is unlikely she would have found the place by herself.

The shuttle slowly began to move, picking up speed as it rolled down the track. Isaac and the other two deviants watched Virginia with an unsettling mix of suspicion and curiosity. With Mary in the operator's room, Virginia felt alone and vulnerable, and she smiled sheepishly as she glanced between the three sets of staring eyes.

Despite the cold and the continuing rain, Virginia felt a pang of relief when the shuttle stopped at another private stop and the door opened. She hurried out before everyone else, looking for Mary.

Mary powered-down the machine and closed the shuttle associate's door. Virginia and the others followed in silence as they trekked through a grove of wild trees. Broken branches were everywhere, the result of nature's wrath against the hapless, unoffending foliage, and a direct path was not clear. Mary led by memory, directing the group through the weatherworn domain, to a clearing marked by two large boulders.

The group continued on, coming to the foothill lining a small cluster of mountains. Mary found the mouth of a hidden cave behind a thick gathering of bushes. The rocky entrance was cold and dark, and Virginia made sure she stayed close behind Mary. Virginia felt uneasy in the darkness, unable to see how sturdy the rocky ceiling really was. She imagined the earth above them collapsing in on the tunnel at any given moment, trapping all of them in eternal darkness, and she hastened her pace. As soon as they wound past the first bend, they could see light, and by the time they found the main cavern, they could feel warmth emanating from an electric heater. Virginia hurried out of the shadows, shivering as she moved into the warm, lamp-lit cavern.

The large, rocky area appeared to be a study and stock room, with shelves of electronics and laboratory supplies on one side and several large and expensive pieces of equipment on the other.

Ray King sat in an ergonomically correct chair in front of a monstrous desk, reading a file on his computer, a personal bodyguard standing on either side of him. He appeared to be in his late thirties or early forties, but Virginia couldn't tell for sure. He didn't have any gray hair, save a few rogue strands in his beard, but his face had a defined character that developed only with age. He looked up as the group dropped their loot, noticing Virginia as the outsider that she was.

Virginia nervously went up to Ray, and the bodyguards moved in front of her path, blocking her with their combined mass.

"Anne sent her," Mary said, pulling coils of copper wiring from her bag, entering them on a catalogue sheet, and then finding their place on the supply shelves.

"I don't have anywhere else to go," Virginia said, surprised to see so much technology. "Medical-Corp told my family that I was dead."

Ray turned to the others in the cavern, save his two guards. "I need all of you in the work room." He handed Anne's lunch box to Isaac. "We have few new tests I need you to prepare to run." He shouted after the others, "and the builders need help wiring the new turbine."

The room emptied, save for Virginia and Ray.

"You're one of the humans infected with the Blue Dust?" he asked her. "The HD-1 virus?" he amended.

"How did you know?"

"I just assumed." Ray downloaded information from the desk's computer onto a smaller, hand-held computer, and then he began to manipulate the figures on the smaller screen with a thin, plastic stylus. He set the hand-held computer back into its synch port and loaded his changes, turning to Virginia with his full attention. He moved closer to her, studying her eyes. "And you were at the hospital?" he asked.

"The virus gave me a terrible fever . . . a lot of other people too, bad enough for over a dozen of us to be admitted within a week or two of one another. When they saw what the virus did, they refused to let us go."

Ray ensured that his previous information had finished loading, and then grabbed his hand-held computer and began to input more figures. "Good that you were able to get away."

"Anne helped me escape."

Ray nodded, looking pleased. "I knew that girl

Leigh M. Lane

would come in handy one of these days."

"Do you know who developed the virus?" Virginia asked. She considered how she might react if Ray admitted that he was actually the one responsible for the destruction of her old life. Was she ready to face the person who deliberately took so much away from her so soon after that loss?

"Some of my scientists developed it, but I have no idea who deployed it," Ray said, scratching his beard. "It was not my intention for the virus to get people killed, or even to infect the random people it infected."

"The virus didn't kill anyone. They chose euthanasia over living out the rest of their lives . . . like this. The hospital was happy to kill them."

Ray added another note to his hand-held computer. "I'm glad to know that. Isaac was adamant that it wasn't deadly. I had my doubts." He chuckled. "I guess that's why I'm the philosopher and tactician, and not the biochemist."

Virginia found herself speechless. Here she stood, stripped of her dignity, her family, a lifetime of earthly possessions, her very humanity, and Ray was bragging about his tactical capabilities. "Why?" she finally asked, unable to find any other suitable response.

"Why did we develop the Blue Dust?"

Virginia nodded.

"Leverage."

Virginia remained silent, confused.

"The people in power are always the ones given the privilege of writing history. Corporate is in power, and it's done one hell of a job trying to keep us under its heel. They've said a lot of terrible things about us over the years." Ray punched in a few commands, and then he showed Virginia the screen. A short video began to play.

The video showed an fMRI and PET scan of a deviant brain compared side by side with a normal human's. Although the deviant brain was indeed smaller, it exhibited about twice as much activity level.

"The dark eyes claim superiority, citing brain size as their only proof," Ray said. "But we are very clearly their intellectual superiors."

"You're insane!" Virginia exclaimed. "If you're so smart, then why are deviants only allowed to work in manual labor and sanitation?"

"So we don't take over the world and render the dark eyes obsolete, naturally," he said, the calmness in his voice almost startling. "But we've learned to use it to our advantage. They're only prolonging the inevitable."

"The inevitable?"

"My goal is to spread awareness, to prove to the dark-eyed population that we are people, too. I have been privately funding genetic research, so that I can gather the evidence I need to prove we deserve our place in society. Nothing more."

"How many people are involved in this?"

"More than you would guess. This cave is the smallest of four bases I run from my computer," he said confidently. "And we're connecting with other groups far beyond our districts. We'll have a network across the entire western half of the country soon."

Virginia looked at all of the stolen items

catalogued and stacked along the walls. Her heart raced as she realized that she was consorting with the leader of what was probably the biggest organized deviant crime circuit on the West Coast. Somewhere under this man's command, the HD-1 virus had been created. Who knew what else he was capable of?

"So, I'm dead to my family and I look like a deviant. What am I supposed to do? Where am I supposed to go? I don't care if you're only inadvertently responsible for my condition, I want to know what you're going to do to help me get my life back," Virginia said, surprised to find her backbone as the words poured out seemingly on their own accord. She could feel her face going red and she turned away from him, fighting tears.

"First of all," Ray began, still remaining perfectly calm, "You don't just look like a deviant—you *are* a deviant. Get used to it. Second, if you think I'm going to pay you some kind of restitution, you can kiss my ass. However, I would be more than happy to employ and house you, should you decide you can live with working for a crazy, pompous jerk such as myself, as well as be willing to bend a few human laws about which you, as a deviant, now no longer have any say. Sound fair?"

She reluctantly nodded, still too angry and upset to look him in the eyes.

"Good. Your first assignment will be to report to Isaac so he can take a sample of your blood."

She almost spoke again, but changed her mind before she said her first word. The situation was enough to make her stomach turn, but what could she do? She'd fallen haplessly into it. Was this how everyone got their start in organized crime? Giving blood one day and deploying genetically engineered viruses the next?

He pointed to a dark tunnel on his left. "Isaac should be in there. If not, come back and we'll hunt him down together. He disappears sometimes. God knows where he goes off to."

Virginia held her breath as she slowly approached the narrow cave. Her heart raced when she entered, as if she might find something terrible within its shadows. Chills rushed through her as she turned a corner and moved through another long stretch of darkness. She considered turning around and fleeing the place, but again it hit her that she had nowhere else to go. It was all she could to do pray for the strength to continue.

Taking a deep breath, she turned another corner and entered the small, dim cave.

# Chapter Fourteen

Faith-Corp owned some of the largest buildings in each district, having coliseum-sized churches and university-sized arrays of schoolrooms for Sunday class. Families registered their attendance at consoles located throughout the main lobby, and seating was assigned each week during check-in. Thousands of people, mostly Corps, pushed and shoved their way through the crowded seating aisles, many of them wearing their stylish new facemasks and rubber gloves, searching to find their seats before the service began.

The worship associates got started on their first set just as George and the kids found their seats. By the luck of the draw, their seats were in the first tier balcony this Sunday, the highest seating any Corp employee could take. It was only a tier below the Corporate boxes, where the well-dressed pillars of society always sat. Corps and Marts rarely saw Corporates outside of church, and so no one knew much about them beyond what they wore each week and who they were seen with most recently. They stood over the masses in their little cliques, showing off their manicured nails and fine tailored outfits, old money descended down from the fat cats of centuries ago. They never looked down at the several tiers of people lined up below them. It was as if everyone else sat behind an invisible wall that only the rich could see, and no one on the outside even existed within their tiny, separate world.

The worship manager invited the congregation to join his associates in song, and the building filled with the echoes of ten thousand voices united. The sound was rich, but it did little to affect the smug sense of detachment among most of the people there. George and the kids were no exception; they were there because everyone else was, and everyone else was there because they didn't want to be badgered by Faith-Corp associates.

The hymn ended, and the worship manager moved his team straight into the next, directing the congregation to continue singing along. The worship manager kept the music going non-stop for close to twenty minutes, making sure he gave the people their full tithing's worth for the week. He silenced his associates, and a spotlight followed the sermon manager from his entrance to the podium.

A clatter of applause thundered through the building, and the sermon manager raised his hands to silence the crowds. He waited for the applause to end, and then he leaned into his microphone. "God told me ya'll would be excited to come here today!" he said, smiling from ear to ear.

There was another small round of applause, but the manager was able to speak over it and snuff it out with his amplified voice: "I want to talk to ya'll today about family values. Normal *human* family values." He looked around, to ensure he had gained the attention of all he could directly see, and then he continued. "Do you see any deviants here today?"

Everyone took an obligatory look around their personal vicinities, although they already knew that not one deviant would be among them.

"I talk to more and more people that think it's okay to socialize with deviants, just because they look so similar to us. Do not be fooled; deviants do not have souls. They are the freak result of a godless science, whose creators will surely go to Hell!" There was a small amount of applause, but the manager continued. "Now, I don't think God wants us to hate them, but He does want us to be responsible about how we approach them. You must remember that they are atheists, every last one of them, and therefore they have no morals. They are a poison to the human mind, toxic to the human soul."

There was another short clatter of applause, and then the sermon manager checked his notes and moved on. "God came to me when I was praying the other night, and He told me that there are human beings in our own congregation living just as sinful of lives as the deviants."

There was a hushed murmur of disapproval.

"I was just as shocked," he continued, "but God told me that He would forgive those people, but only if they repented and showed their devotion to Faith-Corp by sacrificing a tax-deductible, one-time donation of one quarter their monthly tithing before they leave today. Praise God!"

"Praise God!" the congregation echoed.

"God wants us to be happy, but He also wants us to live in accordance with His teachings. Satan is ever-present in society, but that doesn't mean he has to be ever-present in our personal lives. Can I hear you say hallelujah?"

"Hallelujah!" the people replied.

"Our lesson today comes from First Corinthians. Follow me, if you would, to chapter fifteen, verse thirty-three."

Most people had traditional paper Bibles, tattered and old, but many of the wealthier members pulled up the verse on hand-held reading tablets. There was a quick shuffling of pages and tapping of commands on tiny screens, and then there was a hushed silence as the congregation waited for the manager to dictate the verse from memory.

"'Do not be deceived: Bad company ruins good morals,'" the manager quoted. "Do *not* be de*ceived*," he repeated for emphasis. "The Bible dictates that we stay true to ourselves, as both believers and as human beings. It also warns us to be choosy about our associations. Do not be deceived by atheists, intellectuals, and free thinkers, as they will only lead you astray. God is the only truth, and faith is the only path. Amen!"

"Amen!" the people repeated.

The sermon manager gave the worship manager a subtle nod, and another hymn rose up from the stage.

George exchanged glances with Shelly and Kurt, all of them getting anxious for the service to finish. Kurt started fidgeting and growling his frustration. He hadn't understood half of what the sermon manager had said; what boy his age would? Worse yet, a handful of the female worship associates now fought to see which among them could sing their shrill voices the loudest. Meanwhile, the managers stood by the stage door, engaging in a private conversation that only the two of them could hear over the din of singing voices. Whatever they were talking about, the worship manager seemed to think it was very funny.

Shelley grabbed Kurt and sat him on her lap. "Just another minute or so, sport," she whispered.

The worship manager went back to his post as the associates came to the end of their song, and with a wave of his hands, he ended the service.

George stood, turning to Shelley. "Can you get him to his class?"

Shelley nodded.

"I'll meet you both later in the shuttle garage, then," George said, and then he pushed his way into the crowd to rush across campus to his class.

Shelley and Kurt waited for the crowd to thin, and then together they made their way to the long hallway that led to classroom buildings C, D, and E. The lights along the hallway flickered, threatening to go out, somehow continuing to hang on. Kurt held Shelley's hand as they moved toward the building where both of their classes were held.

A news associate stood with a small crowd standing around him, his cashier associate moving past each person with his scan gun. Shelley, still having George's debit card in her bag, dragged Kurt to the news crowd and paid to join the audience.

"These guys are always so boring!" Kurt whined.

"I just want to hear a few minutes," Shelley said,

tightly gripping his hand to make sure he stayed with her.

"Everyone is on high alert, unsure when or if the deviant resistance group will strike again," the news associate began. "Officials urge residents to wear facemasks and gloves when out in public until further notice. Any questions?"

A young woman raised her hand, and the associate called on her with a point of his finger.

"Have any official statistics been released on the number of people who have died from the HD-1 virus?" the young woman asked.

"None at this point, although officials do warn that the virus is deadly and able to live on porous surfaces for several days if not weeks. Anyone with a high fever is to report to Medical-Corp for mandatory quarantine," the news associate confidently replied. "Any more questions?"

The news associate looked through the crowd then continued with his report. "Shuttle delays have been on the rise, mostly due to increasing rain and hailstorms. While Trans-Corp workers are doing all they can to compensate for the delays, they do wish to relay their appreciation for your continued patience. Current construction of additional power supplies, which would allocate more reliable electricity to Transportation-Corp, are still awaiting Corporate approval. Any questions?"

He surveyed the crowd. Seeing no raised hands, he continued, "Info-Corp has received warning that flash blizzards may be only a day or two away. Authorities say you should expect cold warnings in halls and shuttle garages, with nighttime lows of negative twenty. Commuting workers can expect early-leave shifts until the warning has passed. Any questions?"

Shelley raised her hand, and immediately he called on her.

"Can you tell us more about the deviant terrorists?" she asked nervously. "Does the Police-Corp have any leads?"

The news associate shrugged. "Sorry, but we haven't received anything about the terrorist acts since Police-Corp managers opened up their investigation." He turned away from her. "Now on to more of today's news. . . ."

A pair of hands went over Shelley's eyes from behind her. "Guess who?" a young man said playfully.

"Stephen?" Shelley turned to face him, pleasantly surprised to find the familiar classmate standing behind her.

"I haven't seen you in school for a few days. Are you okay?" he asked.

She shrugged.

"Daddy had to move her to the Mart School," Kurt said, making innocent conversation.

Shelley coughed.

"Is that true?" Stephen asked her, shocked.

Shelley nodded, her embarrassment growing so heavy that she felt like she might buckle beneath the weight of it.

"I'm really sorry," he said looking genuinely disappointed. He looked at his watch. "I should get going. I'll see you around." Stephen gave her a short wave over his head as he turned and fell into the moving crowd behind him.

Shelley angrily turned to Kurt. "Why did you have to tell him that? I didn't want anyone to know yet!"

Kurt shrugged. "I'm sorry. I didn't know."

Humiliated and no longer interested in the news, Shelley pulled Kurt by the arm to their building.

"I said I was sorry!" Kurt said.

Shelley dropped Kurt off at the door of his classroom, and then hurried down to the end of the hall.

There were thirty other teenage girls Shelley's age in the room, one of whom was Charlotte. Charlotte and Shelley often had classes together throughout the years, both in Sunday class and in the Corp Education System. They had been friends since first grade, when both of them tested into the system. Charlotte was troubled, but the two of them had fun together growing up.

Charlotte waved her over to a saved desk, and Shelley stared indecisively for a moment before crossing the classroom and accepting the seat.

"Where have you been?" Charlotte asked.

"Long story," Shelley said, her flat voice warning that she was in no mood to explain.

Charlotte shrugged, then she turned to look at the notes already written on the dry-erase board.

Shelley also looked, but the writing was so illegible that she gave up and decided just to wait for the Sunday class associate's lecture. Shelley glanced around the room just as the last of the students were finding their seats. She saw two girls staring over at her, whispering back and forth about the latest gossip. By the way they looked back at Shelley, what they had on her was rich. They giggled, and another girl leaned over to see what all the fuss was about.

Charlotte noticed the girls as well. "What's up with them?"

"Stephen," Shelley said almost under her breath, her throat knotting.

Assuming the scenario was one of kiss and tell, Charlotte pretended to be indifferent about it. "Stephen is a jerk. I wouldn't believe anything he said about you."

Shelley gave Charlotte an uneasy smile. "What do you mean by that?"

Charlotte shrugged. "Live and learn."

The Sunday class associate came into the room, taking a moment to get her materials organized while the students quieted. She took attendance, and then she cleared her throat as the last few voices dwindled.

The two girls gossiping about Shelley continued whispering and giggling between the two of them, and the associate cleared her throat again. This time she was louder, glaring directly at the girls, making her request of their attention unmistakably clear.

"Is there something you'd like you share with the rest of the class?" the associate asked.

One of the girls pretended to try to contain herself, nudging her friend. "You tell them!" she said.

The other girl looked back over at Shelley, who stared back, silent and anxious. Her eyes were wide with fear, begging the girl to let the matter die.

The Sunday class associate sensed that something was amiss, and she picked up her hand-held computer. "Our sermon today was in First Corinthians, chapter fifteen, verse thirty-three. Can anyone refresh the class's memory?"

A handful of students raised their hands, and the associate called on Charlotte.

Charlotte read from her paperback Bible: "'Do not be deceived: Bad company ruins good morals.'"

"Can anyone tell the class what exactly that means?" the associate asked.

The same handful of people raised their hands, and the associate picked on a shy-looking girl in the back row.

"Sometimes you can think someone is your friend, but they're really deceiving you?" the shy-looking girl said, opting at the last moment to turn her answer into a question.

"Close. Anyone else?"

"You're only as good as the people you associate with," one of the giggling girls said out of turn, glancing over at Shelley.

The associate nodded. "That's correct."

Unable to take another moment of the girls' torment, Shelley got up from her seat, bowed her apologies to the Sunday class associate and left the room.

The associate poked her head out the door as Shelley ran down the hall. "Excuse me! Where are you going?"

Shelley did not turn to the woman as she replied, "Back off!"

"I'm going to have to mark you as truant!"

"You do that!" Shelley turned a corner and fell out of sight.

She ran until she was halfway to the shuttle garage. Remembering that she would have to turn around eventually to pick up Kurt when classes were over, she stopped and took a moment to catch her breath before returning to the C building. She stood across the hall from the corridor leading in, trying to decide what to do with herself for the next hour, when Charlotte came out. She could tell by the look on her face that Charlotte was working to digest a heavy load of unwanted information, her face contorting with deep contemplation as she moved across the hall.

"Whatever you're going to say, you can just save it," Shelley growled.

"What kind of fiend do you take me for?" Charlotte asked, looking offended.

Shelley shrugged. She wasn't sure what to expect from anyone at this point. More than anything, she couldn't bear to set herself up for anymore heartache. Clearly, the gossip about her change in status had already moved beyond just Stephen and those two girls. She had to wonder, though, why the news prompted Charlotte to go looking for her.

"You don't need a Corp education," Charlotte said. "I bet my buddy Dean would give you a job right now if I asked him."

Shelley shrugged again, feeling reserved but also wanting to give Charlotte the dignity of some type of response.

"You're good company," Charlotte said. She pointed to the building. "And you're better than all of them."

Shelley nodded, although she knew Charlotte was sugarcoating the situation.

"I should get back." Charlotte grinned deviously. "I told the class associate that I was going to try to bring you back with me, but I'm assuming that's not going to happen."

Shelley gave her a sideways glance. "Do you blame me?"

Charlotte shook her head. "See you around," she said, and began toward the building's main door.

"Hey!" Shelley called across the hall.

Charlotte stopped and turned. "Yeah?"

"Thanks."

"Sure." Charlotte disappeared into the building, leaving Shelley alone in the quiet hall to contemplate the few options that remained in her life.

None looked promising.

# Chapter Fifteen

George and William didn't say a word to one another during the entire shuttle commute. They had acknowledged each other's presence in the garage, each making his boundaries clear, each avoiding eye contact with the other.

George had finally shaved and showered, doing his best to present himself as clean and pressed as possible for the inevitable meeting he would be having this morning with his manager. He tried to think of what he would do if one of his associates missed two days of work due to drunken and disorderly conduct. Would he start the paperwork for position termination, or would he hear him out and consider the fact that everyone made mistakes? He didn't know his manager very well, and the man was painfully difficult to read. George had no idea what to expect, and already he sweated profusely. He looked down with deep embarrassment as he realized he had sweated through the underarms of his shirt, and he quickly buttoned up his jacket in attempt to mask the offense.

The shuttle slowed as it entered the garage. George felt his stomach go sour as the shuttle came to a halt, the passenger doors shooting open, the time to exit no longer simply a dreaded thought in the back of his mind. He watched William leave before him, waited several paces, and then began toward the stairwell that led to his floor. The thought occurred to George to turn around, get back on the shuttle, and see where it led him instead of facing whatever wrath Corporate had approved for him. He knew the penalty for refusing to report for a shift, however, and he wasn't in the mood to return to jail anytime soon, so he cast aside his dissolute thoughts and began up the stairs.

He quickly moved through the maze of cubicles, finding his manager in a closet of an office in the back. The room felt uncomfortably cramped, having barely enough room for a desk and filing cabinet. George felt claustrophobic as he stood across the desk from the tall, lanky man.

"I'm really busy, so let's try to keep this brief, okay?" the manager asked, foregoing the typical formal greeting and handshake.

"Sir, I know that I missed two more days last week, and I know I'm going to get written up for it, but I ask that you consider a few things before you decide whether or not to begin the termination process," George said, wiping the wet, beady film from his brow and upper lip, unable to stop sweating.

"You're George, right?" the manager asked, looking perturbed, but also strangely confused.

"Yes, sir."

The manager pulled George's file from the cabinet, contorting to negotiate the narrow path back around to his side of the desk.

The room suddenly felt even smaller.

The manager opened up the file, glancing over George's history first, and then last week's offense. "You have had, up until this point, an excellent attendance record. Considering the virus going around right now, the fact that you took a few days off for the flu is not going to get you terminated with your current rating. Just try to make sure it doesn't happen again."

Now just as confused as his manager, George tried to figure out how he could get the man to clarify his standing without tipping him off at the potential clerical error. At a loss for words, George knew better than to put his foot in his mouth by pressing the issue any further. He cleared his throat. "Thank you, sir."

The manager added a remark to George's file, a positive note regarding how upset George was over the time he missed, despite the serious fever he sustained throughout his absence. "I'm sure you've got work to do," the manager said, sounding annoyed that George was still there.

"Yes, sir," he said, quickly backing out of the stifling room.

He took a deep breath, feeling infinitely lighter. He loosened up his jacket as he made his way to his cubicle. No one stared at him as he passed by, and no one seemed surprised to see him there. The truth behind his absence had been expunged, although George had no idea who would have gone to such lengths to pay him such a huge favor.

At least now he knew why his Law-Corp file had been temporarily "lost." He still had a friend in this world, even if he couldn't be sure who that friend was.

He sat down at his desk and turned on his small computer. A file associate came by with a fresh stack of partially completed files for George to get started on. With a renewed feeling of complacency, George thumbed through the stack, chose his first case of the day, and got started. Never before had it felt so good to sit in a cubicle.

The report George chose charged a deviant with being caught near human Housing after dark, being out of the home without identification, and lying to a police associate. According to the report, the man tried to persuade the associate that he wasn't a deviant and he'd locked himself out of his home. He had contrived a ridiculously disturbed story in which he escaped from the hospital after the HD-1 virus transformed him, accusing the district hospital of holding him and a dozen others against their will. He even accused the hospital of killing at least half of the patients, and forcing the rest to consent to becoming human-deviant Guinea pigs.

Although the story was obviously contrived, George pushed through the report. Every time he tried to analyze another entry, however, his thoughts took him back to Virginia. Was it possible she'd died to cover up something that Corporate didn't want the population to know? How far-fetched was the deviant's story, really? If it was so far-fetched, why couldn't he stop thinking about it?

George sat back for a moment, unable to concentrate. He tried to collect a quick mental list of the little he did know in hopes that a moment of forced rational thought might help him to clear his head enough to get back work. He closed his eyes and searched his mind: Virginia had been terribly ill; deviants were the result of germ-line therapy, not retrovirus infection; deviants were notorious for lying; George had Virginia's ashes on a shelf in the bedroom. The agony returned as he considered the possibility that the deviant was not lying, and that Virginia was still alive, trapped somewhere in the district hospital.

If the deviant was lying, George wanted nothing more than to beat the man to a bloody pulp for belittling his wife's death in such a careless way. If he was telling the truth, however, George wanted to hear the story straight from its source. He decided to "lose" the deviant's file for the time being, until he had a chance to visit the man in jail. When he would find the time was beyond him, with work and other obligations taking up most of his waking hours, but he knew he needed to meet with the deviant if even just for the catharsis. He wondered how many days the man would end up missing at his job, assuming he had one, because of his arrest. George was determined to make him miss at least a few more.

Ensuring that no one was watching, George took down the deviant's name and case number on a small piece of paper and stuffed it in his pant pocket. He locked the file in a cabinet drawer and moved on to another random file on his desk. He took a deep, calming breath—he had actually gotten away with breaking one of Corporate's strictest confidentiality rules. He had a client's personal information hidden on him, and no one was the wiser. He wondered if

Leigh M. Lane

perhaps the practice was not as difficult and impermissible as he had been led to believe.

George worked diligently through the rest of the day, reading every file with extreme care and triple-checking his work, feeling the need to work especially hard to make up for his wrongful act against the company. He almost threw away his notes during lunch, but he knew he would only end up taking down the information again by the end of the day, so he held fast to his decision.

He needed to see the deviant for himself, to hear the lie about the HD-1 virus with his own ears. He needed to know for sure. . . .

He needed it to be a lie.

# Chapter Sixteen

Virginia had to take a shuttle to the four corners of the quadroplex, and then cross into District 89149 by foot. Wearing a borrowed jacket and a skimpy maid's uniform, she thought she might freeze to death before she found the next closest shuttle garage. The rain had let up for the time being, but the early morning chill had dropped below freezing, the wind sending it straight to her bones and stinging her hands and feet.

She approached the beginning of a hallway system, checking her directions to ensure she had found the correct complex. She entered through a thick metal door, and the three different directions she had to choose from all had signs clearly stating where they led. The hallway to Virginia's right led to Info-Corp's main office building. The hallway to the left led to the North shuttle garage, and the hallway straight ahead led to the central shuttle garage.

Virginia walked straight, feeling shorter and meeker the closer she got to the garage. It seemed as though she was one of the only deviants in the area, and by the looks of the expensive attire and designer face masks the people around her were displaying, she knew she stood out in the large crowd like a black ant on a clean, white counter top. She could feel the eyes on her as she quietly found her shuttle track and sat down.

There was a sudden commotion as every person in the vicinity felt the need to voice his or her surprise and outrage. Virginia looked around, eyes wide and sharp, unsure of what was going on.

A security associate came up to Virginia and pulled her up by the base of her arm. "These benches are for *us* only, miss."

Virginia looked around, her face red with humiliation. "No one else is sitting here!"

"No one else wants your lice, either," the associate said, backing from her, readying his nightstick and waiting for her response.

Virginia did not try to return to her seat, but she did give the associate a piercing glare. "I don't have lice."

"It's just best we don't take that chance," the associate said, holding the nightstick in a manner that suggested he was ready to use it.

Virginia moved away from the bench, waiting by the tall metal sign that marked the 320 shuttle stop.

The security associate followed her. "I'd like to see your papers, while I've got you."

Virginia dug into her large, almost empty bag, and produced several perfectly forged documents. Ray had arranged for an identification card, work papers, and a health certificate clearing her of the newly dubbed "Deviant Typhoid Mary Syndrome." All

papers had to be on her person at all times, Ray
explained to her, especially when traveling through
and working in the rich district. Because there had
been so many terrifying reports about deviant
wrongdoings the past few weeks, Police-Corp was
having its associates looking for reasons to get them
off the streets. With Info-Corp suddenly pegging
deviants as the harbingers of lice and disease, Police-
Corp decided that any deviant found without an
updated Proof of Health Certificate was to be arrested
immediately.

The security associate thought for a moment,
decided that he had nothing on Virginia, and then
handed back her documents. "Everything seems to be
in order. Just stay off the benches." The associate
returned to his post, turning to glance at her every
minute or two.

When the shuttle arrived, Virginia allowed the few
people who came after her to board first, averting
whatever conflict might arise from boarding before
them. She remained standing, grasping a hand-bar,
standing as far as she could from the seated
passengers. She avoided eye contact as the shuttle
carried her and a handful of people to a garage across
the district. To her relief, the shuttle emptied at the
garage, and one other deviant boarded. He also stood
as the shuttle continued further into the richest part of
the quadroplex.

Virginia kept to herself, hoping that the deviant
across the way would remain just as silent. She was in
no mood for small talk. Her feet were killing her, the
uniform was cold and itchy, and she felt that she had
given up almost every last bit of her dignity getting

this far. She couldn't even wear her wedding band for fear of someone accusing her of having stolen it. Was all of this worth it? She was about to betray what her heart told her were still her own people, and for a meager roof over her head and a few warm meals. Would she even be able to go through with it? She had always wanted to meet a member of Corporate. She never thought in any of her wildest imaginings, however, that it would finally happen under such unpleasant and unwelcome circumstances.

Ray had found Virginia a job as a servant for the very prestigious Conrad family. Mr. Conrad was believed to be the top Corporate representative for Info-Corp, and according to Ray's top sources, Mrs. Conrad was a retired mother who now was a full-time member of the National Corporate Logistics Board. Ray told Virginia that both of the Conrads were key players in what he dubbed "the Anti-Deviant Propaganda Campaign," and a keen ear properly planted in their house could prove invaluable.

Virginia would stay at the Conrad estate for four-day shifts, on call day and night while she was there, and then go "home" for three days to catch up on sleep and take care of whatever personal business she might have. Ray made it very clear that her job for right now was to get to know both Mr. and Mrs. Conrad as well as she could, and also mingle with the other help to see what further information she could obtain.

The task sounded simple, and yet it instilled a sense of dread in her that she couldn't shake. She would have been nervous visiting a Corporate even back when she was a "normal" human being. Now the dynamics between them were even more complicated. How would she be able to stand remaining in such a beautiful and luxurious home, knowing that she was now considered such a lowly creature? Even if she was cleaning the place?

Nothing Virginia had heard about Corporate living could prepare her for the actual estate when she got there. The Conrads had their own private shuttle hub, which gave way to a covered pathway leading to their immense front gate. A speaker box was anchored to one side of the gate, and Virginia pushed a large red button to call an attendant.

A young woman's voice crackled through the speaker. "State your business."

Virginia pushed the "Speak" button and moved her face close to the box. "My name is Virginia Ir . . . Virginia Seton. I've come to fill the servant position."

"Just a moment." There was a buzz at the gate, and then it slowly creaked open.

Virginia entered the estate, and she jumped with a start as the gate slammed shut behind her. She walked with awe and trepidation as she made her way across the gigantic yard surrounding the house. There was an immense lawn, and all around there were trees, bushes, and vines. An arbor hung overhead the majority of the path, trained with morning glories, moonflowers, and wisteria vines. Even living in the middle class, Virginia was a young child the last time she saw a private yard, but never before had she seen one this large or elaborate.

Virginia made her way to the main house, climbed up the freshly whitewashed veranda steps, and rang the doorbell.

A young deviant woman promptly answered the door, leaving the protective chain on for the moment. "Virginia Seton?" the young woman asked.

Virginia nodded.

"I'll need to see your papers before I can allow you in," the young woman continued.

Virginia produced the documents from her bag and handed them through the slightly ajar door.

The young woman looked through the documents then handed them back before unchaining the door and opening it completely. "I'll need your bag, Virginia."

Virginia hesitantly handed her the large bag, stuffing her documents in her apron pocket.

"The last girl the agency sent us was a thief," she said. "He swore it would never happen again, but I hope you don't mind if I take extra precautions?"

Virginia shook her head. "I'm no thief. I promise you won't have any problems with me, Miss . . . I'm sorry, I didn't get your name."

"Nadine."

"You won't have any problems with me, Nadine."

"Good." Nadine seemed a little bossy to be a servant, but Virginia remained silent about the matter. Nadine was very pretty, somewhere around thirty, and had long, wavy brown hair that she had tied back with a black ribbon.

"Where do I start?" Virginia asked, hoping that cleaning someone else's mansion would somehow be less tedious than cleaning her own humble apartment. The entry hall was large, with bronze statuettes arranged along the tastefully decorated walls. The entry opened up to an enormous foyer, adorned with small tables holding priceless artifacts from different eras of the past. A tall, thin statuette of the Egyptian goddess Bastet watched over the entire room, the thin, catlike figure serving as a centerpiece for the rest of the display. An antique vase stood not too far away, and an ancient carving of the Earth Goddess sat on the other end of the large room. On the walls to the sides of the elaborate, winding staircase were famous paintings that had likely been auctioned off in some museum's desperate attempt at the beginning of the anti-waste movement to stay in business for a few more months.

"Let me give you the tour," Nadine said, and then began toward the kitchen.

Virginia followed, speechless.

The kitchen was enormous, with more appliances than any person could ever need. It seemed like the entire room was made of stainless steel, and even the walls shone. There was a huge stove with four burners on it and an oven large enough to bake a full-sized turkey. Cast iron pans hung overhead a large, granite-top island, and beside them hung ladles, cooking spoons, and spatulas.

Beyond the kitchen was a storage room, where breads, cheeses, cured meats, and canned goods stood on shelves. Bags of rice and beans were stacked beside a bin of fresh potatoes, and an electric refrigerator and freezer stood in the far corner. A dumb waiter stood open in the middle of the wall on their right, with a small hand-held computer sitting in its transport box.

"We cook all of the meals, although Mrs. Conrad does all of the meal planning. I hope you actually know how to cook," Nadine said.

Virginia shrugged. "Well enough."

Nadine led Virginia back through the foyer, allowing her to peek her head into the game room, which was complete with a pool table and arcade-style pinball game, and the downstairs toilet. "Don't get caught in either of these rooms unless you're cleaning or serving in them, or you'll be in a world of pain."

"We aren't allowed in the bathroom?" Virginia asked.

"We have our own bathroom." Nadine opened another door, revealing a wooden staircase. She reached in and flipped on a light, and a dim bulb flickered to life.

Virginia looked down the staircase, feeling as though she were entering a dungeon. "Our bathroom is down there?"

"Where else would it be?"

Virginia took in her dark surroundings as she followed Nadine down the steps. They turned a corner and passed a small room with two cots, each with a pillow and a single blanket. Just beyond the cots were the bathroom and a small kitchenette area. Beside that was a small laundry area. Virginia saw that the bathroom had a mirror on part of one wall, and she slowly moved to see her reflection in it.

She had not seen herself in a mirror since going into the hospital, and she was surprised to see the deviant eyes staring back at her through the reflective glass. Their color was so pretty and yet so ugly at the same time. Virginia lost herself for a moment, unable to turn away from the image.

"Are you okay?" Nadine finally asked.

Virginia fought to keep her composure. "I'm fine."

"Good. It's time to make the Conrads' breakfasts." Nadine went back up the stairs, and Virginia followed quickly behind her.

Virginia looked up the staircase that led to the Conrads' bedroom. "What about the upstairs?"

"I do all of the upstairs cleaning. Mr. And Mrs. Conrad are very particular about who they allow around their personal business." Nadine gave Virginia a strange smile and then led her back across the foyer.

They returned to the shining kitchen, and Nadine pulled the hand-held computer from the dumb waiter. She tapped in a couple of commands, and then set it back in the transport box.

"Can you use a computer?" Nadine asked.

"I'm sure I can figure it out."

Nadine pulled two frying pans down and set them on the stove. "Mr. Conrad wants a cup of black coffee," she began. "Mrs. Conrad wants two waffles, three eggs scrambled in bacon grease, bacon, of course, and hash browns."

"That's a lot of food," Virginia said.

"I wouldn't offer any opinions about it in front of Mrs. Conrad if I were you. She's very touchy about her eating habits."

"She must weigh a ton," Virginia said.

"I wouldn't use that language around here either," Nadine whispered into Virginia's ear as she walked off toward the storeroom. She disappeared for a moment, returning with eggs, potatoes, and an onion in her apron. She set them on the island, then disappeared again for the batter mix and bacon.

145

"Could you get the coffee brewing?" she asked, setting down the rest of the food. "The grounds are in the fridge."

Virginia retrieved a can of coffee grounds from the refrigerator and found the coffee maker. "I could sure use a cup of coffee," Virginia said, taking in the amazing bittersweet fragrance of the dark grounds.

"No food unless you're on break, and no using the kitchen cups or plates for yourself. I'll show you which ones are yours when we go back downstairs," Nadine said as she took the potatoes and onion to Virginia and handed her a knife. "Peel and chop these up after you get the coffee started. We'll see how well you can make hash browns."

Virginia got to work as Nadine went to the stove and turned on one of the burners. She lined up several strips of bacon in the pan, and soon the sizzling, sweet smell of salted pork filled the room. Nadine put the bacon on a plate to drain, and then she immediately got started on the scrambled eggs. Virginia cringed as Nadine kept the bacon grease hot and dropped the beaten eggs into it. The grease crackled as the eggs cooked, spitting and hissing with the heat. The eggs slowly soaked up the grease, transforming their whites to the colors of caramel and burned toast by the time they were done.

Virginia heated up the other pan and poured a small amount of oil into it. She waited a moment for the oil to heat, then dropped a generous serving of potatoes and onions into the pan. She covered it with a metal lid, and then she returned to the coffee pot and poured Mr. Conrad's coffee.

Nadine loaded the first course onto the dumb

waiter and sent the lift upstairs, ringing a tiny bell. As the bell rang, Virginia froze to hear the screeching bark of a small breed dog.

"What was that?" Virginia asked.

"Mrs. Conrad has a pet dog. Nippy little thing," Nadine said, not fazed in the least bit about the pet.

"Where did she get a dog?"

Nadine shrugged. "I'm guessing that Corporates have some sort of black market that only they buy and sell through," she said, keeping her volume low. She pulled a large bowl from a cupboard and got started on the waffle batter. "It's not like anyone is going to tell any of them what they can and can't do."

Virginia stirred the hash browns, found salt and pepper in the spice rack, and gave the dish a light powdering of both. The sweet smell of onions and potatoes joined the lingering aroma of fried bacon and eggs, and Virginia grabbed her stomach as it began to growl.

Nadine started a waffle, watching as Virginia went to pick a small crumb of egg from the cooling pan. She quickly passed Virginia, pretending to look for something. "Cameras," she breathed before grabbing a container of syrup from the cupboard and setting it beside the dumb waiter.

Virginia stopped herself, instead taking the pan to the sink and scrubbing it down. She set it aside to dry, and then checked on her hash browns again. "How do I know if the potatoes are seasoned properly if I can't taste them?" Virginia asked, feeling justified in her reasoning.

"You'll learn," Nadine said.

The transport box lowered back into the kitchen's

end of the dumb waiter, and Nadine loaded the syrup and a healthy slab of butter.

The steam from the waffle iron soon diminished, and Nadine opened it. The waffle was a perfect golden brown, and Nadine smiled as she grabbed a fork. With a remarkably believable set of movements, she pretended to burn herself as she went to move the waffle to the plate. The waffle went into the air, and she feigned an impressive attempt at saving it before it fell to the floor. "There is one exception," Nadine said, calmly starting another waffle in the iron.

Nadine picked up the fallen waffle and tore it in half. "They both get a kick out of seeing us eat off the floor," she said, handing half of the waffle to Virginia and taking a bite from the other.

Virginia could tell that Nadine kept a clean kitchen, and she ate the waffle without a second thought. "Thank you."

She checked the hash browns as she finished her waffle, deciding that they looked done enough. She arranged them on a large plate and placed them in the transport box just as Nadine slid the second waffle onto another plate. With the rest of the breakfast order loaded, Nadine sent it up with another ring of the bell. Once more, there was a yippy bark in response to the bell.

Nadine finished her waffle then licked her fingers before rinsing them in the sink. "Now it's time to get this place cleaned up," she said, then grinned thoughtfully. "Mrs. Conrad likes to keep a spotless kitchen."

# Chapter Seventeen

George stormed into the dark kitchen with both of his hands up in the air. Kurt had been screaming and crying in his bedroom for two hours, calling desperately for his mother, and George had exhausted every idea he could think of to calm the boy down. Muttering to himself, he sat down beside Shelley, who had spent so much time writing poetry earlier that she was now forced to finish her homework in the dark.

The Mart Education System turned out to be less horrific than Shelley had thought it would be, and despite her initial desire to give up, she seemed to be coming around. She was still reluctant to make any new friends, but she did find the decreased academic pace to be a refreshing mental break. She was scheduled to test for job allocation tomorrow, and she held hope that her many years of Corp education would set her above the other students. If she was going to be a part of the Mart Segregate, she was determined to be the highest-ranking Mart employee there was. Maybe she could even have another shot at a career that involved writing.

"Can you *do* something about Kurt?" George finally snapped, his left eyelid beginning to twitch.

Frustrated and probably even more tired than George, Shelley dropped her pen and went to console the boy. Kurt lay on his bed, crying out in heavy, anguished sobs, and he barely noticed when Shelley entered the room.

"Hey, you," she said, sitting down beside him.

"It's not fair! I need her here!" Kurt cried. "Mommy!" he screamed after working a moment to catch his breath. "Mommy! Please come back!"

Shelley wanted to cry with him, but he needed her strength right now more than her added mourning. "How about I tell you a story?"

"I don't want a story—I want *my Mommy!*"

Shelley tried to think quickly, heartbroken over Kurt's pitiful display. She hugged him as tightly as she could. He continued to scream and cry, but after only a moment, he closed his eyes, calmed down, and hugged her back. He took long, shaky breaths, whimpering here and there, reveling in Shelley's maternal embrace. She wasn't his mom, but she would have to do.

Shelley kept silent and still, afraid that any quick movement might set him off again.

Kurt had acted out in class several times since their mother's passing, refusing to do his work, and even picking fights with other classmates. George didn't know how to discipline him, given what they had all endured throughout the past few weeks, and he feared that the boy was at the beginning stage of a behavior problem he might not be able to fix.

Virginia's death had left a painful void, and he knew that Shelley and Kurt both felt that same emptiness. He didn't know how to fill the void for any of them, and so he convinced himself that going to work and paying for Kurt's expensive education might compensate for at least some of the boy's loss. With Kurt's recent behavior, however, George had to wonder if he was working as hard as he was, only to be wasting his money on educating the wrong child.

It was too late to change his decision now, as reintegration into the Corp Education System for Shelley would be an expensive and lengthy process, despite the fact that she had only just begun to attend the Mart school. He needed to regain control of his family before the legacy he and Virginia had worked so hard for was crushed for good. But how could he convince a seven-year-old to look to the future when he couldn't even help him move past all he was suffering through right now?

There was a knock at the door, and George slowly got up to see who would be rude enough to come by unannounced after dusk. He looked through the peephole, surprised to see William nervously waiting on the other side. Suspicious of William's intentions, George called to him through the door. "What do you want?"

"We need to talk," he said, turning back to make sure Judith hadn't come out behind him.

"What about?"

William impatiently shifted from one foot to the next, and then looked straight to the peephole. "It's about Virginia. I think she might not be dead."

George swung open the door and quickly joined

Leigh M. Lane

William in the hallway, quietly closing the door
behind him. He charged toward William, backing him
into the wall across the way. "What the hell are you
trying to pull?"

"Do you think I'd lie to you about something like
this?" William asked, squirming away from the wall
in an attempt to put some distance between the two of
them.

George had his face right up to William's, and his
breath irritated William's nose as he spoke: "I don't
know what to think anymore! But if either of my kids
hears you, so help me, I'll make sure you hurt as
much as they do over it!"

"She came by on Friday, about an hour before you
got home," William insisted.

"Why didn't you say anything before?" George
growled.

William looked hesitant. With a deep breath, he
looked George straight in the eyes, his face terrified
and sincere. "She wasn't human anymore," he said,
and then quickly added with a flinch, "Please don't
hit me!"

George backed away from William, his thoughts
falling into a jumbled mass. Feeling dizzy and weak,
he backed to the wall on his side of the hallway and
leaned against it to keep from falling over.

Judith came out and stormed over to William.
"What are you two talking about?"

"Nothing!" William quickly said.

"You told him, didn't you?" Her voice went deep
and angry. She turned to George. "It wasn't her!
People don't just turn into deviants!"

With Judith's angry prompting, William went back

into their apartment and the door slammed shut.

George fought to remain on his feet, his legs transformed to gelatin, his knees threatening to buckle. He made his way back into his apartment, bracing himself against the door as he closed it. Searching for the strength, he made his way to Kurt's bedroom to ensure that neither he nor Shelley had heard William's claims.

Kurt slept in Shelley's quiet arms.

She looked up as George came to the door. "Dad, what's wrong?"

"I have an errand I have to run after work tomorrow. Can you pick up Kurt and hold the fort until I get home?" he asked, his voice a hushed whisper.

Shelley shrugged, looking tired. "Is tomorrow macaroni night?"

He patted her on the shoulder. "Can you do me this favor?"

She nodded. "Yeah. No problem."

"I really appreciate it," he said. He felt his pocket and the stolen information, and a strange sense of relief came over him when he felt that the paper was right where he had left it.

Shelley sat up, her eyes blinking away the sleep forcing its way on her. "Go ahead and turn out the bathroom light. I think I'm stuck right here for the time being."

George nodded, and then switched off the dim light.

He moved through the darkness, feeling his way into his bedroom, and then stopped beside the box where Virginia's ashes supposedly lay. He felt the ring that still rested on his left finger, and he fell to his knees. Closing his eyes despite the darkness, he silently began to pray.

# Chapter Eighteen

Job allocation testing had been a breeze, and Shelley was sure that she would be given the option of any Mart job she wanted. Still, she had to wonder why her life had to take such a dramatic turn. She had been a good kid, so why her? It just didn't seem fair that her life should change so drastically, so quickly. She felt tired and overwhelmed, and she feared she might never get used to all of the exhausting changes she had no choice but to incorporate into her new weekly routine.

Kurt waited for Shelley in the garage, just outside the hall to his building, about a yard from the usual security associate. He turned and just happened to see Shelley approaching. He smiled, hurrying to her side.

"How was school?" Shelley asked, quickly leading Kurt to their shuttle track. She looked around, hoping no one she knew was in the vicinity to see her.

Kurt shrugged, his mood suddenly going sullen and quiet.

"What happened?" she asked, already knowing that Kurt was in some type of trouble.

Leigh M. Lane

Kurt dug into his backpack, and then handed a small slip of paper to Shelley. "My teacher says you need to sign this."

Shelley read the notice, which requested parental permission to reprimand Kurt by any necessary means for refusing to do his class work. The class associate added that she had tried taking away privileges, putting him in the corner, and even explaining to him the consequences of failing out of a Corp class, but he still refused to look at his work. The class associate also noted that Kurt had become disrespectful and violent, and she would begin paperwork for suspension if the notice wasn't signed and returned immediately.

"You know what this means, don't you?" Shelley asked Kurt.

"What?" Kurt asked.

"Your class associate wants permission to spank you in class because she doesn't know what else to do with you. Do you want to get forced out of the Corp Segregate, too?"

He shrugged.

She handed the slip back to him. "Dad has to sign this."

He returned the slip to his bag. "I'm not letting some stupid class associate spank me."

"You'll stop misbehaving, and then you won't have to worry about getting spanked!" Shelley said, taking Kurt by the hand to hurry him along. "Dad gives you the Corp life and you just piss it away! What is your problem? Why can't you behave?"

"You're not my mom!" Kurt broke free from Shelley's grip, and then darted off into the crowd.

156

"Kurt!" Shelley ran after him, but she lost his trail quickly amid the sea of other people. She stood near the center of the shuttle garage, unsure where she should go from there. "Kurt!" she yelled again.

The crowd of students and parents surrounding her became one giant blur. She could no longer see any individual faces, only a wall of moving bodies standing between her and Kurt. "Kurt!" she tried again.

She spotted Charlotte and ran over to her. "Charlotte, have you seen my brother?" she asked, nearly too panicked to utter the words.

Charlotte looked around. "I haven't seen him. Are you okay?"

"He ran off!" Shelley cried, still searching in all directions. "He got mad at me, and then he was gone!"

Charlotte looked at her watch. "I've got a little time. We can cover more of the garage if we split up. Meet me at the bench in front of the Line 120 shuttle track in twenty minutes?"

Shelley nodded, and then the two went off in opposite directions.

Shelley went from one end of the garage to the other, seeing no sign of Kurt anywhere. She grew not only increasingly fearful for his safety, but she was also extremely angry with him for putting her through such unnecessary panic. It would take every bit of restraint within her to keep from spanking him herself when she finally did find him. Why did he have to make life even harder, when things were tough enough as it was? Why couldn't he just return to the sweet, well-mannered boy he was before all of this?

Shelley flagged down a security associate, giving him Kurt's description and begging for his assistance. He imputed an alert in a local database, informing all security associates in the vicinity that there was a missing little boy. The associate waited for a response, but no reports came back.

Shelley made another sweep of the garage, even backtracking as far as Kurt's classroom to look for him there. He seemed to have disappeared. She went back through the garage, searching through the crowds, crying and cursing. She made her way to the Line 120 shuttle track, hanging her head in defeat, praying that Charlotte had better luck. When she saw Charlotte waiting for her, with Kurt still nowhere in sight, she felt a heavy knot return to her throat.

Charlotte put a hand on Shelley's shoulder. "I'm sorry."

Shelley shook her head, giving herself permission to cry.

"You've done everything you can," Charlotte said.

"What am I supposed to do—just go home without him?" Shelley said, distraught.

"What more can you do? If he doesn't want to be found, he doesn't want to be found." A glimmer came to her eyes. "I think you should come with me. Dean's friend is having a party tonight. You two would totally hit it off. Maybe you can even talk to him about a job." Charlotte turned as she heard the Line 120 shuttle slowly come in. "You can always leave if you get bored."

Shelley shook her head. "I can't go anywhere until I find Kurt."

"You've got security looking for him. For all you

know, he's already halfway to Housing by now."

Shelley heard someone call her name, but who and from where she could not tell. She turned to Charlotte. "I think he just called for me."

Charlotte gave her a concerned grimace. "I think you need to let the guard associates do their job—and you need to take a few hours to relax and take care of *yourself*."

Shelley saw a woman who looked ridiculously similar to Virginia, and she nearly choked. Her thoughts felt as though someone had pressed a pause button on her mind. Time slowed. The din of voices all around her fell into an echo chamber.

Charlotte waved her hand in front of Shelley's eyes. "Shelley?"

She turned to Charlotte, a contrived smile stretching across her face in an attempt to mask her sudden confusion. "Yeah?"

"Are you coming?"

Shelley surveyed the heavy crowd once more, the question barely registering.

Charlotte took her by the shoulders and steered her toward the shuttle door. "Okay, best friend here is making an executive decision. I can't stand to see you so stressed out. You're coming with me."

Shelley did nothing to resist when Charlotte led her into the shuttle, ignoring little voice in the back of her head that was shouting at her to break off back into the crowd and continue searching until she had Kurt safely in her custody. She took one last look through the crowd before the doors closed, and then she sat down beside Charlotte as the shuttle began to move. A party was the last place she should have been going, but at the same time, the idea of letting go of every responsibility she had accrued, go off to God-knew-where just for one night, and raise a small bit of hell felt like the very thing she needed to get her head back on straight.

Even still, she couldn't get Kurt off her mind. She prayed he had boarded the shuttle to Housing, causing her to search needlessly long after he had left. Hopefully, he was home, safe, waiting for their dad to get home to try his hand at making macaroni and cheese. And if he didn't go home, then what? Would Kurt really run away? Shelley considered how out of character such a move would be for a timid, anxious childlike Kurt, but then she weighed the fact that she was stepping out of character, herself, as she traveled beside Charlotte to party with thieves and black market thugs.

She fought a hot wave of nausea as a flood of second thoughts suddenly hit her. How would she be able to live with herself if Kurt turned up missing, hurt, or worse?

"How's it going at the Mart school?" Charlotte asked, pretending it was no big deal.

"It's not so bad," Shelley said, embarrassed to be talking about it in public. She looked around, surprised when no one nearby seemed to be interested.

"What are the Mart guys like?"

Shelley shrugged. "I haven't really met anyone yet."

"You've been there a week and you haven't met anyone? They're all going to think you have a chip on your shoulder or something."

"I'm pretty sure they already do."

Charlotte nodded her sympathy, and then fell silent for a few minutes. Finally: "Dean's friends will totally dig you. Loosen up a little. We're going to have a blast."

Shelley gave Charlotte her best attempt at a smile, her anxiety growing as the shuttle slowed and Charlotte stood. She followed Charlotte through the garage, to the tunnels leading to the beach path. Both girls had on heavy jackets, the weather having become cold and the sky grey and angry. It was much cooler outside than it was in the halls, but the girls stayed warm enough by moving quickly. They spoke little through the long trek, both of them winded and ready to collapse by the time they finally reached the beach.

The beach was cold and windy, and gusts of sand kicked up here and there as the two moved past steep dunes in search of Charlotte's meeting spot with Dean. A few other people already stood there waiting, and Charlotte ran ahead to introduce herself. Shelley slowly followed behind her, reservations still swimming in the back of her head. She stopped as she got a good look at them. "Charlotte!"

Charlotte tried to back away as she also realized that the three people waiting for Dean were deviants.

"Did you come here to play, little girl?" one of the deviants asked. He brandished a long knife and a serious face.

"They're here for the party," said another, focusing his attention on Shelley. "You friends with the motherfucker that slit my brother's throat?"

"Run, Shelley!" Charlotte darted off toward the

north.

Shelley followed close behind.

"Don't let that bitch get away!" Shelley heard the one with the knife yell.

Shelley shot for the cold ocean, giving herself the last resort of trying to out-swim her pursuer if he got too close. He quickly closed the gap between them, however, and soon she could hear him right behind her.

The familiar sound of the sand-cruisers had her waving her arms as she ran. "Help!"

The deviant gained on Shelley, tackling her to the wet, sandy ground. She thrashed and fought, and his knife went flying before he had a chance to use it on her. The remnants of a wave rushed in and sent near-freezing water over both of them. She fought to get up, but the deviant shot a punch straight to her eye, knocking her back. He threw himself on top of her, pinning her down.

Another wave went over them, and Shelley struggled and choked as the salty water rushed over her face. She dug her nails into his arms, fighting him as he attempted to remove her shirt. He slapped her across the face, stinging her lips, and she fell back with a shriek.

He pulled up her shirt, stopping at her head so that it now served to both blindfold her and pin her arms over her head. She writhed and kicked as the man kissed one of her breasts.

Then, suddenly, he was off her. Shelley screamed as someone dragged her from the waves.

"It's me!" Charlotte said, helping Shelley with her shirt.

Dazed, Shelley watched as Dean fought the deviant in the shallow waves. Dean surprised the deviant with a knife of his own, and he gutted the man with a single, forceful move.

"Your eye!" Charlotte exclaimed.

Shelley felt the swollen mass, her throat going tight.

"You okay?"

Shelley nodded, although her tears betrayed her. She felt dizzy, and she held onto Charlotte's arm as they made their way to one of the other sand-cruisers.

Charlotte helped Shelley onto the back seat, putting Shelley's hands on the driver's waist. "Hold on tight or you'll fly off," she warned.

Shelley held onto the young man's waist, her continued shock over the deviant's punch seizing her trembling body. She turned to Charlotte, wanting to go home, but the fiery redhead had already mounted Dean's sand cruiser. All at once, the sand-cruisers took off toward the north, and Shelley cringed as they passed the dead bodies of the deviants who had chased after her and Charlotte. Both were sliced badly, and the sand beneath them was dark with blood.

The sand-cruisers all came to a stop at the district border, just outside a sizeable crowd of teenagers and young adults drinking and mingling on the beach. Shelley followed, staying as close as she could to Charlotte as the group left their vehicles and joined the crowd.

"Who are all of these people?" Shelley asked.

Charlotte pointed to an older man in the crowd. The man was completely gray, with a receding hairline and a two-foot-long beard. He didn't look like he had the strength to lift a dumbbell, let alone control a group of rowdy, jaded young adults. No one seemed to care that he wore not the conventional pants and polo or blouse, but a toga, a blue and red striped tie, and a cowboy hat.

"Homer will give us all the details as soon as enough people have arrived," Charlotte said, staring over at the man with a measure of adoration Shelley found baffling.

Shelley looked around, apprehensive about what to expect next. A group of people nearby was gathering driftwood for a bonfire, while others were admiring the blood still on Dean's knife.

"Who could have guessed that deviants didn't have blue blood to match their sickly eyes?" Shelley could hear Dean say, flashing the knife so all could see.

The crowd cheered.

A young man produced a Molotov cocktail from nowhere and lit it, sending it into the teetering pile of driftwood. Shelley jumped as an explosion of flame set the bonfire alight. The crowd cheered, and Shelley worked to recover part of her dignity by joining in on the commotion. Someone handed her a bottle and she took a swig, swallowing with a tight grimace.

Homer raised his arms into the air. Before he could speak his first word, the crowd went silent. The waves crashing into the beach somehow became louder, and shadows fell across the mass of people as the bonfire fought to break the darkness that now surrounded them all.

"I see a couple of new faces this evening," Homer

said, surveying the crowd. "It's always good to see new faces. Sponsors, raise your hands, if you will."

Charlotte, as well as two other people in the crowd, raised their hands.

"Come and see me after the meeting," he said, and then quickly shifted his focus back to the entire group. "I just got the latest from a news associate, right before I came here. It seems that the deviants have waged another set of attacks, setting loose another wave of the HD-1 virus and potentially infecting another several dozen innocent human beings. Enough is enough!"

The crowd responded by yelling out in disgust and calling out hateful slurs.

"How many of you have lost loved ones to deviant misdeeds?" Homer asked.

Shelley and a handful of other people raised their hands. All eyes searched through the crowd, tallying the numbers.

Homer hurried over to Shelley. "What did the deviants do to you, my dear?"

Shelley looked around, fighting a new onslaught of tears. Another bottle came to her hands. She took a heavy swig of the moonshine. "They killed my mother!"

"And you would like to see the deviants responsible pay for what they did?" Homer asked, his tone implying that he already knew her response.

Shelley nodded.

Homer turned toward the rest of the crowd. "Who else would like to see them pay?"

The crowd cheered.

"Why hasn't one deviant been arrested for these

murders yet?" Homer continued. "I'll tell you why—because Corporate is incompetent! What other choice do we have but to take matters into our own hands?"

Shelley wiped tears from her eyes, hoping no one saw them as they threatened to spill over onto her cheeks. What she heard terrified her, but it also made some sense. Why wasn't Corporate controlling the deviant problem better? If people had acted earlier, might her mother still be alive today? Did she really have any choice but to stand up for what was right and put the deviants back in their place? Still, in the back of her mind, Shelley had to wonder: Was it okay for a person to feel so hatefully vindictive?

"I need three groups of ten," Homer said.

Everyone, save Shelley and a couple of the other new faces, raised their hands.

Charlotte, who eagerly had her hand up, nudged Shelley. "Raise your hand!"

"What are we volunteering for?" Shelley asked, still hesitating.

"We'll find out when he's briefing us." Charlotte grabbed Shelley's hand and put it in the air.

Her overwhelm suddenly became too much, and the reality of all Shelley had seen and done that evening hit her nearly hard enough to knock the wind out of her. She pulled her hand back and began to back away. "I . . . I need to see if Kurt got home! I've got to go!"

Charlotte followed as Shelley hurried down the beach. "Come on, Shelley! Stay just a little longer!"

"I shouldn't have come here!" Shelley cried as she continued south along the shore.

"You know Homer is right."

Shelley refused to turn back, but she also felt the need to say, "I know."

There was the sound of a motor starting up in the distance, and within moments, Dean caught up to the girls on his sand-cruiser.

"Is something the matter?" Dean asked.

"Shelley's just getting cold feet," Charlotte said.

Shelley shook her head. "You don't understand. I left my brother—"

"Let me give you to a lift back to your end of the beach," Dean interrupted, his voice strangely pleasant. "Homer said he'd see you next week, no hard feelings. It's obvious you have been through a lot."

"But the party!" Charlotte sulked.

"Go ahead. I'll be back soon," he said, then he motioned for Shelley to get on the seat behind him.

Shelley got on, still feeling uncertain. She grabbed Dean's shoulders when the cruiser started moving, and it zipped across the beach, toward her end of town. She shuddered as, once more, they passed the bodies of the deviants Dean and his friends had killed. Her mind flashed back to their attack. Her eye was almost completely swollen shut, and it hurt to try to focus. She wondered if she would be dead right now had Dean and his friends not shown up when they did.

Dean stopped at the appropriate landmark. "See you around, I hope."

Shelley dismounted the vehicle. "Thanks for the ride." She turned to start her trek to the tunnels leading to Housing, but she paused when he did not immediately drive off.

"Charlotte tells me you're looking for work," he said. "Is that true?"

She turned back, surprised. "Maybe."

"What kind of work are you looking for?"

She shrugged. "I . . . guess I'd like to find some kind of writing job."

He stood motionless for a moment, watching her, suddenly looking just as perplexed as she did. "Well," he finally said, "I don't think I can get you anything like that immediately, but with your pretty face, I could probably get you into an entertainment job of a different sort." He raised a brow.

"I need to get going," she said then ran off toward the distant tunnels before he could respond.

He didn't follow her, and yet she felt her anxiety grow the closer she got to home. Why did it seem she could never catch a break? Her thoughts began to play against her. What would she do if Kurt hadn't returned? Their father was probably beside himself, and Shelley was sure she would get an earful no matter where Kurt happened to be. She felt her swollen eye, the skin stinging as she touched it, and she cursed her poor judgment. She made her way along the dark trail, and it began to snow when she got about halfway to the shuttle garage.

As the snow began to stick to the ground, the dark trail got slightly lighter and made it easier to follow. Shelley had on neither a hat nor a scarf, and she wore thin-soled shoes. She shivered, keeping up her pace despite the combination of pain and numbness that began to weigh down her feet.

By the time she got to the shuttle garage, she was positive she had frostbite. As she moved through the slightly warmer tunnels, the feeling slowly returned to her toes, and she stopped for a moment as a hot, burning sensation shot through her recovering nerves.

She froze as she heard footsteps coming up from behind her. Not wanting to chance the possibility of running into a security associate—or worse, another deviant—she continued down the hallway as quickly as her aching feet would take her. No one gave chase, but she still felt compelled to run the rest of the way to the shuttle garage. The garage had few people left in it, and the last few shuttles of the evening were boarding. She hurried to catch the last shuttle to Housing.

# Chapter Nineteen

George sat in the dark kitchen, frozen with indecision. His interview with the deviant in the file played over and over in his mind, interrupted every few minutes by a moment of worry over Shelley and Kurt.

The deviant was young, with short curly hair and an unkempt face. He sat across a short table from George, with a security associate watching by the door. He was skinny for a male deviant of his age, as most of them bulked up quickly from the manual labor they typically worked. George's initial impression was that perhaps the young man was a job-deserter. Now, he wasn't so sure.

"I was a programming associate for Power-Corp before the HD-1 virus changed me," the deviant insisted.

"And what were you doing snooping around Housing after dark?" George asked him, shaking both because of the quick drop in temperature that settled in late in the afternoon and because talking to this deviant, knowing he would be discussing Virginia, had his nervous system in overdrive. George glanced over at the wall heater, wondering if it was even on.

"I was just trying to get into my apartment!" The deviant said, his face sincere. "My human identification was taken away from me when they admitted me to the hospital. Same thing with my keys. I was locked out of my own apartment! Why won't anyone believe me?"

George scratched his head. "Maybe because you're a deviant?"

"Fine. Okay." The deviant stood. "I guess we're done, then?"

George stayed where he was. "Would you be able to identify any of the other patients?"

"Most of them," the deviant said, feeling the stubble along his chin.

"Do you remember a woman named Virginia?"

The deviant nodded. "Around your age. Pretty features. I remember her."

George rolled his eyes. "Why don't you tell me something about her that you can't just pull out of your ass?"

The deviant thought for a moment, and George was sure he would simply admit he had been lying and send him on his way. Instead, he took a deep breath and looked George directly in the eyes. "Her favorite color is blue. She has two kids—a little boy and a teenaged girl. She's a regular card shark in both Blackjack *and* Poker, good enough to kick my ass, anyway. Is that enough for you?"

George blinked hard, his breaths getting caught in his throat.

The deviant crossed his arms. "Same Virginia

you're looking for?"

George sat back for a moment, trying to digest this new scenario without getting sick to his stomach. He still wasn't over grieving Virginia's death, and now there was actually a chance that she was still alive. The conflict of information was enough to make his head spin.

"You know, I might even be able to help you find her. Maybe I can help you figure out where she went," the deviant added.

George's heart pounded. "What are you saying? Where would she go?"

The deviant shrugged. "I've got a fifty thousand-dollar bail order that needs to be filled. Get me out of here, and I'll tell you anything you want to know."

George dove across the table, knocking the man to his back, grabbing him by the front of his shirt. He tightened his fist and threatened to punch. "Tell me now—*what* do you know?"

The deviant cried out, cringing at George's tight fist. "There was a riot in the quarantine room! A few of us got out. I think I remember seeing her run off, but it all happened so fast!" The deviant looked over at the security associate, waiting for some assistance.

The security associate glared back, not looking at all concerned with George's threats against his prisoner.

"I don't know anything else!" the deviant cried. "You have to believe me!"

George backed off, straightening his shirt. He gave the young man a hateful glare and quietly fled the cold cell, feeling more lost than he had been when he had first come. He weighed the different possibilities.

It was feasible that the deviant was nothing more than a con man looking for someone to bail him out. He could have gotten information about Virginia from somewhere else . . . but how could he possibly have known in advance that anyone from Law-Corp, let alone George specifically, would be coming to question him? He couldn't have.

If what he said were true, would Info-Corp willingly withhold such an important detail from the public? Would Info-Corp even be let in on such a dirty secret? The deviant's story fit way too closely with the one William had relayed before, and the more George thought about it, the less he was able to accept it as a simple coincidence. Perhaps he was still in denial over Virginia's death and was distorting facts to suit some twisted fantasy in the back of his head.

And then he had to consider another whole new question: if Virginia was alive, would he still want her if she was a deviant? Would Corporate even allow them to stay married? He thought about the kind, generous, beautiful woman he had married, and he decided that if Virginia was still alive, he would find her. He would see for himself whether she was still the woman he loved. He had even more questions now, and he felt as though he might lose his mind if he didn't find a way to get all of them answered soon. He had to know now, with the utmost of certainty, whether or not he was being played by hateful and selfish lies, or whether he and his family had been deceived by some ridiculous Corporate cover-up.

His family. . . .

There was still no sign of Shelley and Kurt at

home. George wondered if he might have been a little too hard on both of them as of late, and maybe they'd decided to stay out past dark to teach him a lesson. Maybe their plan was to make him worry just long enough for him to realize he wasn't being as much of a team player as he could be. If that was the case, they were succeeding beyond their wildest dreams.

Deciding that he had the scenario completely figured out, he went to his bedroom and packed an overnight bag. He bundled up for the cold, putting on a heavy jacket, his warmest boots, and a protective hat. He found a good picture of Virginia and tucked it into his bag, then he left a note in the kitchen, telling Shelley to keep an eye on Kurt for the weekend. He said nothing about Virginia in his note, not wanting to get their hopes up, telling them instead that he would explain everything when he returned.

He had no idea where he was going to go, but he felt that initiating a physical search would be a far better use of his time than staying idly where he was. He had the weekend to travel the district, and Shelley was old enough to watch Kurt for a couple of days. His decision was rash, but there was too much at stake for him to do nothing.

He locked up the apartment and took off toward the shuttle garage, hoping he wasn't too late to get a quick lift closer to the heart of the district. He ran as a shuttle going northeast was getting ready to begin toward its final trip to the Food-Mart. He boarded the shuttle just in time, and it accelerated out of the garage just as Shelley's shuttle came in.

SHELLEY HURRIED to the apartment, positive she

would freeze to death if she didn't get to a heated space soon. Half of her body felt numb, and everything that wasn't numb burned from the cold. Her head was so cold she could barely think. She still wasn't sure what she was going to tell her father about Kurt, as a huge confrontation the moment she stepped through the front door was most likely unavoidable. Still, she had nowhere else left to go but home.

Much to her surprise, she opened the door to a cold, dark, empty apartment. She felt a warm rush of relief at first, but when she read George's note and realized Kurt was still unaccounted for, another heavy surge of guilt and worry hit her. She turned the wall heater back on and stood by it for a moment. If Kurt was still out in the shuttle garage or one of the pedestrian tunnels, he had to be freezing. Would he have it in him to persevere through the cold just long enough to get back home?

*I need to go back out,* she thought. *I need to find him.*

She thought about the many security associates she'd either ducked past or convinced not to ticket her for being out past curfew. Someone had to have crossed Kurt's path by now. Moreover, if she hadn't seen him anywhere on her way home, what were the chances she'd see him upon a second sweep over that same area?

It was just too cold for her to go back out, she decided. She would regain her bearings and get a good night's rest before returning to her search for Kurt. She would get up early and start back at the Corp Education System's garage, giving his picture to all of the security associates in the area. Hopefully, he just went home with a friend and she could track him down before George got back. Trying to convince herself that she had done the right thing by returning home, that there was nothing more she could have done for him, she tried to get comfortable on the hard kitchen chair.

Not satisfied with how quickly the coils were heating, Shelley decided to take a quick, hot shower. She hurried to the bathroom and turned on the battery-powered light. She looked at her battered face in the mirror, horrified at the sight of her bloodshot eye. Dark bruises were beginning to form all around it, and the swelling still had not let up. Forcing herself to look away, she turned on the shower as hot as her skin could take it. She turned on the water recycler, planning to stay in as long as it took to warm her body clear through. Standing under the heavy jets of water, relishing in finally being warm, she did not hear the telephone ring.

KURT STOOD, shaking and chattering, in a phone booth at the Corp Education System's shuttle garage. He had hidden in the boys' bathroom earlier, when Shelley had been looking for him, and clearly he had stayed in there for a little too long. The game had ceased to be fun some time ago, and now he just wanted to go home. Shelley had his shuttle pass, and he had been denied passage even on the promise that he would pay later. Security sent him on another round of hide-and-go-seek, and by the time he emerged from his spot behind the garbage cans, the entire garage had been shut down for the evening.

Heavy gates kept him from entering school grounds, and he had no idea as to where any of the pedestrian access halls led.

He realized that his hands and fingers were turning shades of red and blue, and he rubbed them together in attempt to warm them. The motion was painful, despite the fact that most of both hands had gone numb. His face and ears had all gone numb too, and his toes felt like frozen rocks in his shoes. As the area became dark and quiet, monsters formed in the shadows. He held perfectly still, even holding his breath when he felt they were particularly close.

As the time passed, he became increasingly certain the monsters stalking him had to be the same ones that had taken away his mother. While he might have sought aid from the random security associate who passed through every hour or so, he dared not move, lest the Boogeyman snatch him out of the darkness and send him into some hellish oblivion. He wished he were in his bedroom, near the dim light of the bathroom, safe at home with his family. He knew running and hiding from Shelley had been a mistake, the repercussions having become far worse than a few harsh words or even a spank on the rear. He wondered if Shelley was now in trouble, too, for having lost him, and he genuinely regretted his childish behavior.

His fingers and toes began to get worse, and he curled up behind the trashcans in attempt to get warm. To his relief, he stopped shaking and he began to feel strangely warm, although his teeth still chattered. He took quick, heavy breaths, the cold air stinging his lungs. His arms and legs became difficult to move, and he stretched periodically to check that his limbs were all still intact. Finally, he tried to get up, only to find that he could not. He stared ahead, watching his frozen breath as it exited his mouth in tiny puffs. Each breath disappeared nearly as soon as it came, and still he became fixated on the tiny clouds. He began to imagine them in fun and different shapes: a star; a heart; a soft, white teddy bear; endless ocean waves; his mother's beautiful, sad, lonely face. . . .

The desire to sleep came on slowly, and then suddenly he had no choice but to close his eyes and rest his heavy head. The chattering stopped and his body fell awkwardly limp. His mind slipped to a warm, happy place where his mother held him in a tender, loving embrace, a place where there were no more worries . . . no more monsters or freezing cold or crushing despair, just him sitting in his mother's arms beneath the comforting glow of a slowly fading afternoon sun, lazily picking out the shapes in the drifting clouds.

AFTER A SHORT, restless night, Shelley made her way back through the pedestrian halls. She could hear rain beating down overhead, and the tunnels themselves were cold and musty. A wave of warmer air rushed toward her when she neared the Corp school shuttle hall, and although the heated ventilation system was set on low for the weekend, it was enough to chase away the violent shivering that had taken hold during her long walk.

As soon as she cleared the tunnel, she paused at the sight of a Police-Corp shuttle speeding in.

A security associate spotted Shelley and ran to

intercept her. "I'm sorry, miss, but this tunnel is closed."

"But I need to get through here."

"What business do you have going through here during the weekend?" he asked, subtly glancing over at a random work of Graffiti on a nearby wall.

She felt a tremble return to her hands. He could take her in if he wanted, and it seemed evident that a crime more serious than graffiti was behind the numbers of officers that continued to file in. She needed to get through, though. She'd already checked in the direction of the Food-Mart, and her only other guess was that Kurt had been picked up and taken to the Safe House while a police associate or two investigated his post-curfew wanderings.

"Miss?"

She bit her lip, hoping the truth might unbar her path. "My brother never came home last night and I was hoping to retrace his steps. I think my dad may have been out all night looking for him and—"

"What does your brother look like?" the associate asked.

Shelley took a deep breath. "He's seven, brown eyes, sandy blond hair."

He nodded. "I think you should come with me."

She found his expression unreadable, and a heavy feeling came over her. "Why? What's going on?"

"Please just come with me."

Her throat grew tight as the man escorted her through the garage. "What is it?" she asked, although she'd begun to suspect the answer.

And then there it was: a tiny, ice-blue limb peeking through the small swarm of police associates.

Shelly collapsed to her knees with a shriek, her body suddenly too heavy for her muscles to carry. Everything went fuzzy, tears blurring her vision. The voices that echoed through the hall became a confusing mass of noise, her own screams adding to the chaos.

A police manager ran up to her and the associate. "What's this?"

"I think we have an I.D.," said the associate.

"I don't know what we'll do with it. Corporate hasn't sent over any work orders yet," said the manager.

Shelley looked up at the two men, then back over at the body. Denial hit her just as quickly as the initial blow, and she shook her head. "No . . . it can't be him. It can't."

She forced herself to her feet. A dizzy spell threatened to take her back down, but she pushed through it and began toward the body.

"Hey!" The security associate tried to stop her, but she darted past him.

Shelley fell into fitful sobs, pushing through the small crowd, as she recognized Kurt's face. His eyes were closed and his face peaceful, his arms tightly locked around his legs. She'd done this. She'd left him to die. She tried to push through to his side, to embrace the body and maybe find a salvageable spark of life remained, but an officer grabbed her by the arm and held her back.

"I'm going to have to ask you to go with—"

"That's my brother!" she cried, yanking her arm from his grasp. She went limp as two more associates moved in to help the manager pull her from the scene.

"Kurt!"

Their voices faded into the din as the police associates spoke:

*We're going to have to detain you if you don't calm down. . . . I can wait with her for a work order if you want. . . . Might need to get higher management involved in this one. . . . Mine's not on call. . . . Neither is mine. . . . We'll just have to wait then. . . .*

*Calm . . . work order . . . not my job . . . we'll neither for do your do my your down down down.*

*Calm down. Calm calm. . . .*

*Miss?*

She became cognizant of her surroundings as the associates stopped dragging her, seemingly intent on keeping her contained at the farthest tunnel connection. It felt so cold there now.

"We're going to need to ask you a few questions," one of them told her.

Shelley thought to respond, but instead she sat, silently weeping, unable to take her eyes away from the body's location. She watched for breaks in the mass of workers . . . waiting for another morbid glimpse of his frozen limbs.

"Miss? *Miss?*"

# Chapter Twenty

Virginia startled awake with a horrified gasp, sitting up in her cot in a panic. Sleep had thrust upon her mind a terrible nightmare, but what the nightmare had been about she could no longer recall. She took a moment to reoriented herself with her new surroundings, having forgotten that she had dozed off in the basement room after the Conrads had retired for the night. Staring at the dark, dreary walls, she felt a sudden, intense longing to be home with her family, missing them now more than ever.

She stood up, shaking off the cold sweat that covered her body. She looked over to the other cot, noticing that Nadine was not there. She made her way up the stairs as quietly as she could, and then carefully opened the door to the foyer. Seeing and hearing no one, Virginia crossed to the kitchen. There was a service light on over the sink, and Virginia saw that there were two used wine glasses sitting on the counter beside an open bottle of Merlot.

Knowing Mr. and Mrs. Conrad would have rang the bell if they had wanted wine, and Nadine would have cleaned the glasses immediately if she had somehow heard the call and served them without waking Virginia, she wondered if perhaps Nadine was just as much the thief as the girl she had just fired. There was a commotion in the storeroom as a few canned goods fell from a shelf.

She tiptoed over to the storeroom, hoping to see something she could use to put that bossy woman in her place. As she peeked through the doorway, however, she found Nadine and Mr. Conrad together on the floor. He had his undergarments down to his ankles, and she was on her back with her legs wrapped around his wrinkled, fat, gyrating body. Neither expected the intrusion, and both were oblivious to Virginia's presence.

She hurried back downstairs, deciding to feign ignorance over the matter for at least the time being. She returned to her cot, but found herself too restless to fall back to sleep. The longer she lay there, the harder she found it to get comfortable. Nadine came downstairs after a short while, and Virginia held her eyes closed, falling still and silent. She listened as Nadine quietly slipped back to her cot.

Virginia told herself she would be extra loud when she cleaned out the pans in the morning if Nadine woke with a hangover. She shuddered at the thought of a man as undesirable as Mr. Conrad making a pass at her, and wondered why a pretty young thing like Nadine would give in to his advances like that. Virginia would just as soon quit than add Mr. Conrad to her list of responsibilities, she told herself, disgusted with just the thought of ever seeing that man naked again. Seeing Nadine with him like that took her already diminished respect for the girl down even a few more notches.

Nadine began to snore and Virginia lay awake, wishing the day would just come so she could get it over with all the sooner. The hours passed by slowly, however, and by the time morning came, Virginia had dark circles under her tired, puffy eyes. She dragged herself off the cot as the morning bell rang, perking ever so slightly when she saw Nadine wince at the light and hold her aching head.

"Time to make breakfast?" Virginia asked.

"We have fifteen minutes to put ourselves together," Nadine mumbled. "If you brew us a fresh pot of coffee, I'll owe you whatever favor you want."

"I'm going to hold you to that." Virginia started a pot of coffee in their tiny, downstairs coffee maker, and then turned to the sink to wash her face. She looked at herself in their small bathroom mirror. With her blue eyes and tired face, she could barely recognize the reflection that stared back at her. She quickly turned away before the image had a chance to induce another untimely surge of emotion.

The basement room filled with the aroma of fresh coffee, a luxury Virginia had not enjoyed for a while. She found two clean mugs and poured a generous serving of coffee for each of them. Seeing no sugar or creamer, she handed Nadine her mug and sat back down on her cot. The coffee tasted rich and bittersweet. Virginia lost herself in the comforting liquid as she slowly sipped at it, reality going on hold until her mug came close to empty.

"We should get to the kitchen," Nadine said, putting on her apron and slipping into her shoes.

Virginia followed suit, getting dressed and combing her hair with her fingers while she followed Nadine to the kitchen. There wasn't any trace of the wine bottle, nor the glasses from the previous night.

Nadine went to the dumb waiter, removing the hand-held computer and retrieving the order for the morning. She moved around the kitchen nervously, barking orders all over the place as Virginia tried to fill her part of Mrs. Conrad's massive order. She held her tongue and did as she was told, understanding that Nadine possibly had a considerable amount of influence through Mr. Conrad and was best not crossed at this juncture.

"You're doing it all wrong!" Nadine grunted as Virginia started preparing an omelet. "Chop up the onion a little finer . . . and you have to slice the cheese thin!" She demonstrated, making paper-thin slices of cheese with her knife. "Like this, see? Have a little pride in your work!" She moved out of the way, wiping her hands in her apron, shaking her head as if she had a reason to be frustrated while she motioned for Virginia to continue.

Virginia took over the cheese, emulating Nadine's ridiculously thin slicing technique, and then chopped the onions until she had reduced them to fine shards. She added them to the egg already sizzling in bacon grease, and then threw in bits of bacon and pepper. Her mouth watered, the aroma of the different foods blending as they cooked together, and she considered dropping the omelet to the ground when she was finished making it. Unfortunately, Nadine had it off the pan and on a plate before she could summon up the courage.

Mr. Conrad had sausage and eggs with his coffee this morning, while Mrs. Conrad had two omelets, hash browns, bacon, sausage, ham, and a half dozen slices of buttered toast. Two slices of toast and two liberal slices of ham somehow found themselves on the floor, and Virginia and Nadine helped themselves to the spoiled food, smiling and waving up at the camera to add to the show.

The telephone rang, and Nadine left to the foyer to pick up the downstairs line. "Conrad residence," she said.

One of the Conrads' Corporate managers screamed so loudly through the receiver that Virginia could hear him from the kitchen door: "Get me either of them, and make it fast!"

"One moment." Nadine put the man on hold and paged the Conrads' bedroom. She went to hang up her line, and realized that Mr. Conrad's conversation with the manager was still audible. She saw that the foyer camera pointed at the bulk of the artifacts displayed, and not the telephone. Placing her hand over the mouthpiece, she quietly waited to see if either could tell that she was eavesdropping. She kept quiet as the conversation commenced, seemingly without either party suspecting Nadine's presence— just as Nadine had no idea that Virginia was watching her.

"Yes?" Mr. Conrad coughed, sounding annoyed to have had his breakfast interrupted.

"We have a situation," the manager said, sounding nervous. He cleared his throat. "We've got another couple hundred people in the hospital with suspected or confirmed HD-1 infection. What's worse is dozens of deviants are claiming to be displaced humans, and honestly we've lost track of how many people have fallen victim to this thing."

"How many people in Info-Corp know about this?" Mr. Conrad asked.

"Nobody below upper management," the manager said.

"Keep it that way."

Nadine could hear Mr. Conrad explain the situation to Mrs. Conrad as the manager awaited further instructions. Mrs. Conrad grabbed the receiver. "I want a board meeting with our top Corporate representatives. Register us for a time slot around noon, and have lunch available. I'll be at my office in about an hour if you want to meet me there."

"Will do," the manager said.

"See you then." Mrs. Conrad hung up, and Nadine quickly hung up her line. Virginia slipped back in as Nadine hurried into the kitchen. Virginia washed the last of the pans, preparing for the stack of plates that would soon come down through the dumb waiter. Knowing it was best to mind her own business, she pretended not even to notice Nadine returning to the room. Nadine did not say anything to her. She moved directly to the dumb waiter and tried to look busy while she waited for the breakfast dishes to come back down.

They finally came, and the women silently worked together to get them moved and washed. They began to hand dry what they could when Mr. and Mrs. Conrad came walking in.

Mr. Conrad looked even older in the kitchen light, with graying hair and unsightly jowls framing his long face. He wore an expensive suit and hat, but fancy clothing was not enough to mask the worry imprinted deep across his face.

"Is there a problem, sir?" Nadine asked.

"We have to go to the office for a while," he said, impatiently digging his designer facemask out of his pocket. "Mrs. Conrad wants you both in the basement until we get back."

Nadine set down her towel, motioning for Virginia to do the same, and the two crossed the foyer to the door leading downstairs. As soon as they were both on the steps leading down, the door shut behind them and they could hear the click of the lock. Nadine turned on the dim light, and they both went down to the basement room.

"How often do they do this?" Virginia asked, the locked door digging up a touch of post-traumatic stress. She sat down on her cot, sweating despite the cold.

"They go out whenever there's a big issue that requires them to meet with the directors' board, once or twice a week, and then they also leave for a couple of hours every Sunday to attend Faith-Corp's weekly Sermon. You'll get used to it," Nadine said. "At least we both can have another cup of coffee." She went to the kitchenette area and poured them each a second serving. "It's not hot anymore, but it's not completely cold yet, either." She handed Virginia a mug before sitting down on her cot.

Virginia sipped at her coffee, unable to shake the anxiety she felt over their confinement. What if, by chance, a fire broke out upstairs? No one would be there to let her and Nadine out of the basement. They would be trapped. Virginia labored her mind to remember whether or not she had turned off the Conrads' coffee pot.

Nadine noticed Virginia's increasing anxiety and gave her a reassuring smile. "Enjoy your coffee. We'll be out of here sooner than you think." She savored her coffee, seemingly unaffected by their situation.

Virginia set down her coffee mug and curled up on her cot. She closed her eyes, hoping she might find a way to sleep through whatever next few hours they would be down there.

"Don't get too comfortable," Nadine said, pulling a couple of pins from her hair and quietly moving up the stairs. She listened through the door for a moment, to be sure the Conrads were gone, and then started working on the lock.

Virginia sat up, suddenly not so sure how desperate she was for her freedom. "What are you doing?"

Nadine tripped the lock in less than thirty seconds, obviously having performed the act countless times in the past. "Come with me."

"What if we get caught?"

"We won't. Trust me!" Nadine hurried out.

Not really trusting the young woman, but too curious to stay behind, Virginia followed. She entered the foyer and froze when Nadine began up the staircase. "Are you crazy?"

"They won't be back for hours. The HD-1 virus has made another appearance, it seems, and Corporate is officially freaking out." Nadine waited for Virginia to get to the top of the staircase. "Now for the real tour," she said with a mischievous smile as she led Virginia to the Conrads' closed bedroom door.

"What about all of the cameras?" Virginia asked, looking around and spotting two, then three that had likely caught them already in their act.

"I'll reset the recorder as soon as we get to the control panel."

The little dog began to bark, pawing at them from the other side of the door, and Nadine put her leg through the threshold to block the hyperactive animal while she opened it. "Be careful of the dog. If he gets out, it'll take us an hour to get him back in here."

Virginia had only seen a few dogs when she was younger. Corporate had passed a law decades ago against keeping private pets, as they sapped precious resources. Mr. and Mrs. Conrad didn't seem too concerned with the law, however, and Virginia had to wonder how many other laws rich people were allowed to violate. Were they above all repercussion? Was that the true meaning of wealth?

Virginia closed the door behind her, and the toy poodle bounced around her in a tiny fit, smelling her feet and barking at the unfamiliar scent.

"He's harmless," Nadine said.

Virginia ignored the dog, marveling at the beautifully furnished room. The bed's immense headboard was made out of real wood, and layer upon layer of down and thick silk flooded over either side of the king-sized mattress. There was another painting on one wall, and several closed-circuit video screens on another. The Conrads could see every room in their house, as well as a view of the basement door, the outside gate, and the front and back porches, from their bed.

"Why all the hardware?" Virginia asked, already getting annoyed with the incessant barking.

"Mrs. Conrad is paranoid. She thinks the world is out to steal her precious collections of things," Nadine said, a hint of disgust in her voice. "She doesn't trust anyone."

Nadine opened a door that connected the bedroom to an immense office. Virginia hurried in with her, and they got the door closed before the annoying little dog could follow them in.

Various system monitors, computers, and hand-held devices filled the room. The equipment all looked well maintained, and most of it was on. Nadine sat down at one of four desks in the room and logged onto the computer.

Virginia watched intently as Nadine opened an Internet browser window. "The Internet crashed thirty years ago!" she said, trying to figure out what Nadine was doing.

To Virginia's surprise, a web page slowly loaded.

"This isn't the Internet," Nadine said. "Only a handful of quadroplexes are connected."

"What about everyone else?"

"I don't think there is anyone else," Nadine said.

Virginia gave Nadine a suspicious face. "Pardon?"

Nadine logged into the Conrads' e-mail account, accessing newsletters that only members of Corporate were supposed to see. Nadine got up from the chair and offered it to Virginia. "Take a look."

Virginia sat down, and Nadine showed her the basics of negotiating the database.

"How did you learn to run all of this?" Virginia

asked, looking over the various headlines, all arranged by date.

"I've worked in this house for a long time," Nadine said, redirecting Virginia's attention to the computer. She pointed to several decades-old newsletter headlines, which painted a very clear picture of the widespread destruction, all kept from the public, that had occurred all across the country. It seemed that, shortly after worldwide communications completely broke down, communications throughout the country had followed suit. The cause of the growing breakdown was due to more than just the change in weather patterns. In reality, only a small portion of the population still survived. The extreme weather, coupled with the waves of antibiotic resistant disease, had decimated nearly every continent.

Virginia read the headlines in disbelief, and then she sat back, shaking her head. "Why is everyone being led to believe that the rest of the world is still out there if it isn't?"

"It would be difficult to control the people if they were in hysterics over the actual state of the world," Nadine said as a matter-of-fact. She commandeered the mouse and scrolled closer to the top of the page, to the more recent newsletters and correspondences. She opened a recent notice concerning the first HD-1 virus outbreak. Virginia read with a newfound interest. The notice, which was actually a personal letter written from one Corporate to the rest, detailed Medical-Corp's preliminary report on the retrovirus. The report followed the first dozen initial infections, logging the length between infection time and deviant shift, keeping a tally of the euthanasia deaths as if they were inventory adjustments.

"This is insane," Virginia said, finishing the letter.

"You haven't seen anything yet."

Nadine pulled up a recent newsletter, sent from Medical-Corp's top representative:

Header: HD-1a Currently Under Development
Security Clearance: Red
Body Text: Preliminary tests have shown promise in the development of a new retrovirus based on HD-1. HD-1a specifically targets DNA altered by HD-1, causing cell death and eventual death of the host. Further tests need to be conducted, but there is the possibility that HD-1a could target germ-line deviants as well. HD-1a has shown so far to be virtually harmless to the base populace, causing mild flu-like symptoms in some.

Virginia finished reading the newsletter, remaining speechless for a minute or two afterward as she took in the severity of the situation.

"I wonder how many of us they plan on infecting?" Virginia finally asked.

"They can't possibly want to get rid of all of us," Nadine said. "We make up a quarter of the population . . . and everyone else has grown too adverse to manual labor. Someone has to keep rebuilding all that the weather continuously knocks down, you know."

Virginia turned to look Nadine in the eyes, her face heavy with concern. "I sincerely hope you're right." She looked back at the headlines, reconsidering her initial negative impressions of

Nadine. Still feeling suspicious of her sudden sisterly behavior, however, she had to ask, "Why are you showing me all of this?"

"You don't find it interesting?"

"I find it very interesting."

"So why wouldn't I show you?"

Virginia smiled sheepishly. "I thought you hated me," she said with a shrug.

"I'm your boss," Nadine said, smiling back. "But right now, we're both off-duty."

# Chapter Twenty-One

George moved slowly through the shuttle garage, exhausted but still determined. He wandered all night through the entire central area of the district, showing Virginia's picture to anyone willing to look. His body had gone stiff from the cold and every joint in his body ached, but he kept moving. He began toward the Corp Education System's garage just before dawn, when the once quiet, empty garages and halls began to fill with late morning weekend commuters.

He thought that perhaps Virginia might secretly try to see the kids, and if she did, somewhere close to school would be the logical place for her to camp out. She could find them through the crowds and watch them from a distance, disappearing quickly if she was spotted. She also had access to food and water here, but unfortunately, unlike in the immediate Food-Corp area, the garages were not heated at night. Unless she had on layers of heavy clothes, she wouldn't be able to survive the freezing temperatures for long.

George knew that the chances were slim he would

spot her there, but his assumption that she would join the small homeless population in the hallways outside Food-Mart had proved incorrect and he was running out of ideas. Where else would she go? Where else could she go?

Having lost his shuttle pass sometime during the night, likely to a sly homeless person who pretended to be interested in Virginia's photo, George took the pedestrian tunnels across the district. The walk from the central area to the Corp Education System's buildings took him the better part of the morning.

Because of the time and the day, the garage had a comfortable flow of people moving through it. George approached every person he passed with Virginia's picture, but no one seemed to recognize her. He checked the restrooms, but they were cold and empty. He checked every bench, every adjacent hallway, and with every security associate, with no indication whatsoever that Virginia had been in the area anytime recently. Unsure where to turn next, George sat down on a bench to rest his weary feet.

He considered turning back early, weighing the slim possibility of actually finding Virginia against the threat of frostbite and the potential repercussions of leaving his kids for the weekend. Determined to spend at least a day or so searching, reminding himself that Shelley was a capable babysitter, he got back to his feet and began walking toward a random hall.

He noticed a small crowd back by one of the trash bins, with a handful of security associates struggling to keep order.

"Move along!" The security shouted, doing their

best to redirect onlookers away from the scene.

George tried to get a look, but the crowd was too dense. He moved on with a shrug.

As he continued to wander through the pedestrian tunnels, he had to wonder more and more: Had he lost his mind? Did he actually think he could find one person in a district of tens of thousands, on foot, within one or two days? The only two areas he really knew well were those around Law-Corp and Housing, as he normally didn't have much of an incentive to travel anywhere else. Now, while he ventured into unknown territory, he had to wonder if he was going more to satisfy his stubborn resolve than to find Virginia. He was looking for something, although he wasn't certain of what exactly it was.

He walked for miles, stopping to rest when he found himself in an unfamiliar shuttle garage. A few of the shuttles had snow on them, and cold gusts of air flew through the expanse as outbound shuttles left and incoming ones rolled in. George crossed the garage, continuing through to another random tunnel.

About a mile down the way, George noticed that the lights overhead were flickering, which confirmed his fears that the weather was getting worse. Just as he mused that the lights might actually go out forever, every single light in the tunnel blinked out. He froze, the total darkness creating a sheet of black nothingness before him. He carefully felt for the nearest wall and inched his way forward.

He made it through most of the tunnel when he saw a tiny light far off in the distance. The frozen air rushing in toward him told him that the tunnel led to an outdoor path. The cold bit at his nose and cheeks, and he lowered a ski mask over his face before wrapping a thick scarf over his mouth and neck. He noticed the stench of rotting trash as he got closer to the end of the tunnel. He stopped, frozen in indecision for a moment, and then decided to turn around.

George suddenly froze as he heard someone running from the other direction. "Hello?" George called out, bracing himself for the potential impact.

"Out of my way!" a young man yelled.

George flew to his back as the young man ran into him at full speed. "What's your problem?"

"Don't go that way!" the young man warned, out of breath. "Something . . . flooding the garage . . . through the ventilation system! I think it's that disease!"

George quickly turned around, more willing to face the cold and the smell than the prospects that came with the HD-1 infection. Even with his face covered, and even though he saw no glitter floating in from the distance, the fear of becoming a statistic alongside Virginia was enough to make him feel vulnerable and anxious. He reached the mouth of the tunnel, bracing himself for both the stench and the cold while he entered the blizzard.

He gagged as he realized he was at the border of what appeared to be acres upon acres of trash. Plumes of smoke rose in the distance, likely from several fires that smoldered from deep within the various piles of junk. He spotted the young man and followed him, dragging his feet through knee-high snow, down a path between the massive trash heaps.

The young man was not suitably dressed to face the extreme weather conditions, and he slowed down quickly. Shivering and breathing hard, he desperately gathered up a small pile of trash and attempted to light it with matches produced from his pocket. The wind blew out every match he lit, however, no matter how much he tried to shield it, and he began to cry. He turned to George just as he attempted to pass the boy. "I'll give you whatever you want for your jacket!"

George brushed past him. "Sorry. It's not for sale."

The young man tackled George, sending him into a frozen pile of trash. He pinned him down, threatening to punch him. "Give it to me!"

George grabbed both the young man's arms, shifted his weight, and wrestled his attacker onto his back. "I don't want to fight you," George said as he attempted to back off peacefully. With a quick knee in his gut, George dropped to the ground, balling up.

The young man fought to remove George's jacket from him, tugging and kicking with an abject, rabid fervor. George froze for the moment, clinging to his jacket, unsure how to get away. After a minute, however, the young man backed away, stumbling in a panic over his numbing extremities.

"Help me!" the young man cried out, his throat going hoarse from the cold air.

George continued down the trail, ignoring the young man's cries until they faded into the wind.

The trail went straight for a while, and then it forked off into two trails angling about forty-five degrees in either direction. George contemplated the two directions, wondering if there was any significance to the simple choice laid out before him: should he go right or left?

The wind howled and the snow continued to whip through the air. George kicked a heap of accumulated snow off each heavy boot, wiggling his toes to make sure they still could move. He began to shiver, despite his many layers, and he quickly chose the left path, for no other reason than the fact that he had to make a choice. He had to keep moving.

The snow suddenly came down in sheets, and the path quickly became even more difficult to negotiate. The heavy gusts slowed his steps, and every layer of clothing on him soon grew wet and cold. The air bit at his throat, even through the cover he had over his face, and his eyes threatened to freeze shut every time he blinked. Shielding his face with his arms, he continued. The smell of smoke began to grow as he moved down the snow-covered path, and a new sense of hope arose in him with the prospect of a nearby fire. If he could warm himself up for just a few minutes, he thought to himself, he would surely have the strength to reach the other side.

George stopped, feeling overwhelmed as he came up to what appeared to be a dead end. Smoke rose from the top of the massive trash pile ahead of him. Deciding to make a path of his own to reach the fire, George began to climb the pile. His foot sunk into something mushy and his gloves quickly became covered with remnants of decayed food and other unidentifiable muck. He slipped through the trash, unable to gain a foothold beyond a yard or so up in the pile. It was simply too unstable to climb.

He sat down in the snow, his situation suddenly feeling hopeless. He could try to turn around, but how far would he get going the other direction? How many more forks and dead ends were there for him to weave around before he finally reached the other side? And what was on the other side? Was it worth going through all of this trouble? If he backtracked toward the pedestrian tunnel, would he be able to avoid the HD-1 threat?

George became frozen in his indecision, his thoughts feeling clouded and dulled. The cold stiffened up his joints, and they ached as he tried to get back to his numbing feet. His mind reeled, the cold suddenly becoming unbearably hot. He fell back, too tired to continue.

"Help!" George called out, realizing he was succumbing to hypothermia.

George tried once more to get to his feet, but he was only able to stumble another step before he collapsed onto the side of the towering trash heap. He closed his eyes, and darkness came as the blizzard offered to provide him a blanket of fresh snow.

# Chapter Twenty-Two

Shelley thought she had caught a glimpse of George before the security associates dragged her to the mouth of the adjacent tunnel. She had called to her father, waving her arms, but he must not have heard her.

"That was my dad!" she cried to one of the police associates. "You have to get him back!"

"I'll see what I can do," one of the associates said, then hurried off.

Shelley waited for the man to return, frozen in her grief, her mind locked on that one terrible thought: Had she refused to go with Charlotte to the beach, had she continued to search through the night instead of waiting until morning, he might have survived. Something had told her he was there.

*Why hadn't she listened to her gut?*

Medical-Corp took Kurt's body away, leaving her a crumpled, crying mass staring across the garage floor. The shuttle disappeared down the south exit hall, sparks of electricity dragging behind it, and Shelley stared as if it might come back again, just long enough for her to say one more final "goodbye." No one returned, however, and so she sat, alone in the crowded garage, trying to decide whether to bother going back home.

Her father had invested everything he had left in Kurt. How was he going to react when he found out that his only son, his legacy, the Irwin name, had frozen to death while in her care? Granted, he had abandoned them for the weekend, but Shelley knew that wouldn't make a difference. He might even accuse her of killing him on purpose in some crazed, jealous rage over of the boy's education.

"I shouldn't have gone home without you!" she cried aloud. "I should have kept looking!"

"Then you both would have died in the cold," said a woman who sounded eerily like Virginia. Shelly looked around. The garage had once again been opened to weekend foot traffic, but no one seemed to be addressing her. Had her mother's ghost come to console her?

"Where are you?" Shelley cried out, desperate to find the face to her phantom speaker. "Show yourself!"

A few people turned to her, looking surprised and alarmed by her outburst. She listened silently for the woman to say something more, but nothing came. Shelley hurried through the thin crowd as the shuttle to Housing inched its way in. She found a seat, then waited for the shuttle to gain momentum. It moved slowly through the heavy snowfall, and the lack of adequate interior heating left even complete strangers huddling together as they awaited their stops. Shelley stared out the frost-clouded windows, watching what she could of the storm. She happened by chance to spot a giant snowflake as it smacked against the window closest to her, holding its shape for a moment before it melded into the growing sheet of frost, and she couldn't help but wonder how something so beautiful could also be so terribly destructive.

Her cheeks grew raw with tears, her nose red and sore. She couldn't shake the image of Kurt's frostbitten face from her mind. His eyes had been frozen closed. She wasn't sure how she would have reacted if he had stared back at her through that frozen face. Still, what was left of him seemed more like a wax doll than her brother . . . completely inanimate, as if it had never been alive at all. It left Shelley with an emptiness that she couldn't define. It felt almost as if a small piece of death had forced its way onto her soul, threatening to turn all that was left of her foul and grey.

She fought to keep from hyperventilating as her mind's eye brought Kurt's face back to the forefront, only this time he stared right at her, his brown eyes glassy and still. She cried out, and then shuddered at the realization that every person in the shuttle was staring at her. She took slow, deliberate breaths, turning to her window and ignoring the whispers.

The shuttle strained to continue despite the storm. The power threatened to go out a few times, the lights failing through the last several miles of Shelley's ride. By the time the shuttle got to her exit at Housing, she felt ready to collapse. She cried off and on, her eyes so puffy from tears and injury she could barely see. She made her way home, planning to stay just long enough to calm down, warm up by the heater, pack some extra clothes, and gather a few provisions. She tried to call Charlotte, hoping her parents might let her stay with them for a while, but no one answered. After much deliberation, knowing that she absolutely could not face her father's response to Kurt's death, she decided to go to the church for the night, meet up with Charlotte in the morning at Sunday class, and then figure out the rest of her plans from there. She hurried back to the shuttle garage, only to find all of the shuttle associates leaving their posts.

She hurried up to a nearby security associate. "What's going on?" she asked.

"Corporate's given the order for everyone to stay indoors until the storm lets up," the associate said, overseeing the small crowd of people as they hurried toward Housing. "You should go home, miss. Most of the shuttles are powering-down because of the blizzard."

Shelley looked around, hoping to find just one shuttle that was still manned.

"You look like you've been crying. Are you okay?" the security associate asked, glaring at her black eye.

She nodded.

"Then you should return home," he said. "You're liable to freeze to death out here."

Shelley frowned, although she knew the associate was right. She readjusted her bag over her shoulder and began the short walk back home. Frustrated, she started crying again. She rushed back to her apartment, afraid that someone else might see her in such a panicked state, and she hurried through the door and locked herself in once she reached it.

The apartment was just as dark and lonely as it had been before. She stomped over to the wall heater in the kitchen and turned it back on before it had a chance to cool. In a fit of rage, she punched the wall beside the heater, and then pulled back her hand with a defeated cry. She massaged her scuffed and swelling knuckles, suddenly feeling positive that she hated just about everyone and everything. There was nothing left for her here, nothing at all.

Shelley could remember a time when life offered such mystery, such excitement. The world was filled with all different kinds of vibrant colors and fantastic smells, childhood wonders to explore, marvels to discover. As the years went by, however, the colors seemed to fade slowly into shades of grey. Her parents progressively taught her that dreams were the musings of fools, that hope could only take a person so far. No one was above the system. They provided well enough for Shelley and Kurt, but the best they really could offer either of them, when it all came down to it, was a life of mediocrity.

Was she willing to spend the rest of her existence as a manager at the Food-Mart or an assembly line or some other menial crap job somewhere in one of the Mart districts? No . . . whatever did remain of her spirit would certainly wither away if that was all she had to live for.

Maybe death was the only viable option she had left.

Sobbing, she started a hot shower. She forced herself to face the mirror, staring, looking for something—a glimmer of hope, the will to rise above this pain, a desire to continue on. Nothing came, however, and so she gave herself a spiteful sneer. The bruise around her eye now featured giant splashes of yellow and green, making her face all the more unsightly. As she stared herself down, the eyes in the mirror seemed to take on a life of their own. They stared back at her with disgust and hate, egging her on. Crying aloud, Shelley picked up a shaver from the sink. She carefully removed the razor and set it in the shower soap dish.

Removing only the first couple layers of clothes, Shelley hurried into the shower and allowed the hot water to douse her hair and body. A shiver went through her as she sat down and allowed the water to beat down on her. Her thoughts went to Virginia and Kurt, to her broken education, and to all of the new responsibilities that had been dropped down upon her. Kurt's face returned once more, and she screamed and cursed until the image retreated again to the back of her mind. She breathed in the calming steam, telling herself nothing mattered anymore. Her hands shaking, she held the razor up against her wrist.

She closed her eyes, afraid that she might go hysterical at the sight of so much of her own blood. She took a deep breath, trying her best to steady her hands. She pressed the razor hard against her skin, swallowing what she told herself would be the last of her tears, but she could not bring herself to finish the deed. She thought to give herself a moment, and then try again.

She took another mental inventory of all that had gone wrong in her life, knowing that her resolve to end it would return as soon as she thought enough about all of her grievances. Instead, thoughts of a new purpose in life flashed through her mind, and she set the razor blade in the soap dish as she considered her vindictive idea: If she was going to die, she might as well take out as many deviants as she could first. Someone had to suffer for all that she had lost. Someone had to be held accountable. Perhaps she wouldn't get the deviant directly responsible for her mother's infection, but one way or another, she would find a way to even the score.

She got out of the shower, stripping off the wet layers, quickly drying off, and putting on multiple layers of clean, dry clothes. She wrapped a towel on her head, and then went back to the kitchen to prepare something to eat. Saturday was usually chicken pot pie night, but Shelley decided that tonight, for a change, she would have spaghetti. Filling a pot of water to boil, she dug out the spaghetti and canned sauce from the cupboard.

She sat by the wall heater while she waited for her dinner to heat, shaking her hair out of the towel and letting it air dry close to the glowing coils. She glanced over at a small window, seeing nothing through the glass but snow and darkness. The desire to write hit her, and she scrambled for a pen and paper. The release came quickly, the cold, dark words falling from her fingers to the page in thick, hateful waves. She wrote too quickly to keep her penmanship completely legible, scribbling line after line of cryptic, syncopated promise. She stopped for a moment to review her new masterpiece, carefully reading each line. Fully satisfied with the draft, she decided to self-publish. She turned around, took a deep breath, and then wrote her entire poem across the wall in large block letters:

> The dim light flickers overhead
>    and she contemplates the night
>    with vengeance on her mind
>    and a specter's cold hands
>    tight around her throat.
>
> The cold consumes her
>    in more ways than one;
>    thorns and heavy bags of ice
>    only feed the fire within her
>    and draw the demons ever nearer.
>
> The white snow washes out the dark sky
>    only to be trampled and defecated on,
>    reduced to black mud on the ground;
>    what was once white and pure
>    is bound to corruption.
>
> The light flickers out
>    and she prepares herself,
>    knowing what must be done;
>    the specter slowly loosens its grip
>    and she takes a deep, hateful breath.

She finished it with the most professional-looking signature she could manage, and stood back to admire her work.

"Genius," she whispered aloud, tears streaming down her face. "Pure genius."

# Chapter Twenty-Three

The basement had grown especially cold, although the snowstorm had finally ended a few hours ago. The sky remained cloudy and ominous up until the Conrads decided to retire to their bedroom, prompting Virginia and Nadine to retire as well. There were a few small, one-foot-tall windows in the basement, but all of them were close to the ceiling, right above ground level, and snow covered them completely. Virginia stared at them anyway, pretending in the darkness that she was gazing out at the clear night sky.

Both Virginia and Nadine shivered beneath their blankets, both of them too cold to fall asleep.

Unable to take the cold any longer, Nadine grabbed her blanket and got up.

"Where are you going?" Virginia asked.

"The kitchen floor has got to be warmer than this," Nadine said, and then she disappeared up the stairs.

Virginia wasn't sure how the Conrads would react to finding the both of them on the floor in the morning, and she decided to play it safe and stay where she was for the time being. The rest of the house was much warmer, with central heating vents pushing hot air through every room, but almost none of the heat trickled down into the basement. It hardly seemed humane for the Conrads to expect their hired help to sleep down in an unheated basement. Virginia already understood, however, from her earlier findings online, that Corporates were anything but humane.

Virginia thought about the old headlines addressing the state of the world, how the weather was able to deliver the finishing blow disease could not, how only Corporate knew that probably ninety-nine percent of the population had been wiped out, and that stockpiles were running low but nothing was being done to increase current resources. The little that was left of society was being run by madmen, Virginia realized, and she had to wonder, with her new deviant mind, if she would have been as capable of understanding the severity of the situation had she still been human. If humanity couldn't save itself, then perhaps it was time to see what kind of job deviants could do.

She needed to get back to Ray, to relay to him as many of Corporate's headlines as she could remember. Likely, his intelligence already had most of the older information, but the development of HD-1a was relatively recent, and Virginia feared that Corporate might have plans to initiate a mass-release of the new virus very soon.

She thought about the long walk from the Line 320 shuttle to District 89148, knowing that the current weather conditions would make it close to impossible to cross the expanse, especially given her limited wardrobe. For the time being, it seemed that she was trapped.

Virginia heard a scream come from upstairs. Too afraid to investigate, she stayed where she was, quietly listening.

"How could you?" Mrs. Conrad cried.

"I was just curious!" he pleaded. "You have to believe me! It's not what you think!"

"And what do I think?"

Mr. Conrad stammered, skipping through a few unconnected words before going silent. Finally, he cried, "I love you! You know I love you!"

There was the deafening sound of gunfire, three consecutive shots. Nadine screamed.

"Do you have any last words, before I blow your brains out too? Maybe an apology for soiling my husband's body with your vile, filthy, disease-ridden touch?" Mrs. Conrad yelled.

"I'm sorry!" Nadine cried. "Please don't kill me!"

Virginia winced at the sound of another shot, followed by the thump of a body collapsing onto the hard tile. Footsteps stormed up to the basement door, and it flung open. Leaving the light off, the steps creaking beneath her shaky feet, Mrs. Conrad slowly made her way to the basement.

Virginia scurried beneath the staircase, hoping the shadows would offer her more complete cover. She watched from below while Mrs. Conrad eyed the empty cots then frantically turned around to survey the room.

"Virginia?" Mrs. Conrad called, her voice tense. She shivered as the cold basement air bit at her pampered skin.

Virginia struggled to control her panicked breathing, sure Mrs. Conrad could hear her. Her heart beat so hard she thought Mrs. Conrad might be able to hear that, too, and she stared through the shadows, hoping that, by some miracle, she might not be detected.

Mrs. Conrad began to check every possible hiding spot within the room, starting with the laundry area, then the bathroom and kitchenette, and then the staircase. Virginia looked around for a potential weapon as Mrs. Conrad slowly approached her.

"Peek-a-boo!" Mrs. Conrad said, Virginia becoming just visible as her eyes better adjusted to the dark room.

Knowing she would only have one chance, Virginia made a desperate dive for Mrs. Conrad's legs, knocking the woman to the ground. The gun went off, and the heavy kickback knocked it from Mrs. Conrad's unprepared hand as her head hit the concrete. She fell against it with a considerable amount of force, and she fell unconscious with an angry grunt. Virginia backed away, watching the woman for a few horrified seconds, and then hurried up the staircase. She locked the door, unsure whether Mrs. Conrad was dead or still alive, but not planning to stay long enough to find out.

She ran to the front door and flung it open, quickly closing it as a gust of cold air rushed in. She looked around, frozen in indecision for a moment, and then ran up the staircase to grab a jacket from Mrs. Conrad's closet. She opened the bedroom door, and the little dog came running up to her, sniffing and barking. No longer caring whether the creature got loose, she left the door open and found Mrs. Conrad's closet. It was as large as Virginia's entire apartment, with a whole row dedicated to heavy jackets and boots. Every piece was tailored to perfection, many of them sporting heavy animal pelts, exquisite jeweled buttons, and matching accessories such as necklaces, hats, and scarves.

Virginia grabbed a long, heavy coat, which came with a matching hat and pair of boots. She covered her nose and mouth with a thick, cream-colored scarf, and then snagged a pair of dark, black-rimmed sunglasses on her way out. She found Mrs. Conrad's current purse and rifled through it, pulling out her shuttle pass while she descended the staircase to the foyer. She got to the front door just as Mrs. Conrad regained consciousness and tried the locked basement door.

"Let me out, you dumb-eyed bitch!" With an angry cry, Mrs. Conrad began to shoot at the lock.

Virginia hurried off, dashing for the shuttle hub. Seeing no shuttles approaching from either side, she chose a direction and simply began to run. She could find her way back to Ray, she rationalized, as soon as she was beyond the range of Mrs. Conrad's gun. She hurried down the road as far as her legs could take her, terrified that at any moment she might glance behind her and find Mrs. Conrad taking aim.

MRS. CONRAD emptied her remaining bullets into the lock, finally getting it to crack. She yanked open the door and looked around, jumping with a start as her tiny poodle came running up to her, looking for attention. She picked up the dog and gave the house a quick search, although she was already certain that Virginia was gone.

She went to the office she had shared with Mr. Conrad and booted up the main computer. She logged onto the Internet and sent a quick note to the rest of the Corporate community:

Header: HD-1a Dispersal Proposal
Security Clearance: Red
Body Text: The deviant resistance group is planning a massive strike, which could potentially result in Corporate take-over. Mr. Conrad has already fallen victim. They shot him in the head. I fear for my life. I have uncovered plans for the assassination of every other top Corporate official, as well, but I cannot pinpoint all of the individuals involved. I propose Corporate begin the paperwork necessary to begin dispersal of HD-1a, taking a proactive approach before it is too late.

Mrs. Conrad sent the letter to everyone on the Red Clearance List, then sat back for a moment with a twisted smile. She returned to the bedroom, carrying the revolver over to Mr. Conrad's side of the bed, ignoring the dog as it jumped up and begged her for attention. She sat down, opening the nightstand and digging around for the box of spare bullets. She loaded one bullet, and then took a deep breath as she pulled back the hammer. She closed her eyes tightly, taking aim, her trigger hand amazingly calm. The sound of the explosion struck her ear as a hot, stabbing pain lashed through her right temple, but the pain and ringing only lasted for mere seconds before she collapsed, senseless and still.

The poodle yipped at the loud sound, running out of the room for a moment. A heavy ringing sieved through the otherwise complete silence. The little dog pulled her tail tightly between her legs, slowly padding back into the bedroom. Mrs. Conrad's body slumped awkwardly against her husband's pillow, the smoking gun still in her hand, the hot barrel resting against her expensive pantsuit. The little dog didn't know what to make of the sight, and so she curled up on the bed beside the pair of twitching feet.

# Chapter Twenty-Four

George slowly came to, unsure of where he was. He lay on the ground, with a flat pillow beneath his head and a worn quilt over his sweat-glazed body. He appeared to be in a teepee, although he wasn't exactly sure how that could be. The area was warm, with a fire pit in the center and a hole in the top of the cone-shaped ceiling for the smoke. A small cauldron sat strategically arranged over the fire, and a dark brown soup boiled and spat within. George couldn't decide whether it smelled good or disgusting, and he repeatedly sniffed the air to reassess his indifference. His stomach growled heavily just the same.

He sat up, noticing two deviants sitting across from the fire. Presumably husband and wife, they were probably in their mid-thirties, although their hands and faces were worn far beyond their years. They wore rags, and both of them kept their greasy hair unusually short. They seemed deeply engaged in a game of chess, using random household objects as the pieces and an old checkerboard they'd clearly dug up from the trash. The wife was the first to notice George was awake, and they both got to their feet as she motioned the news to her husband.

The two slowly approached George, keeping their distance until they could assess his character.

George tried to stand, but his body felt as if it had been hit by a shuttle. Every muscle hurt, his head pounded, and his extremities felt like they were on fire. He sat back, unsure of his company, but unable to do much about it for the moment.

The woman fetched a water jug and offered it to George. "You must be thirsty."

George was hesitant, but his mouth was so dry his tongue stuck to the roof of his mouth. He stared longingly at the jug for a moment, and then decided that he didn't care what type of poison or disease was in it. He snatched it from the woman and drank quickly, choking as he tried to swallow too much at once.

"I'm Joseph, and this is my wife, Amy," the man said. "We heard your call for help. By the looks of things, I'd say we found you just in time. You fell into a fever, and—"

"My eyes!" George tried to get up again, opting instead to lean in toward the two. "What color are my eyes?" he asked desperately.

"Brown," Joseph said, confused.

George sat back, relieved.

Joseph and Amy exchanged glances.

"Maybe the fever hasn't quite broken?" Amy asked.

Joseph shrugged.

George looked around, wondering how far the

couple had traveled to drag him out of the trash piles. They had to be near the dump. Given the cold and the wind, his call for help couldn't have traveled beyond the pile he had attempted to climb, and he noticed he was surrounded by a strange mixture of clutter. While trash seemed piled around them on all sides, with boxes and bags lined up along the walls, there were also stacks of books, discarded paintings, and a small telescope. "Where am I?" he asked.

Joseph and Amy exchanged another quick look.

"This is our home," Joseph said. "You're welcome to stay here until the weather's cleared."

George closed his eyes. "I was in the dump."

A large, grey rat emerged from a crack in the wall near the floor, and Amy quickly spotted it. "We could use another rat, Joseph! Quick!"

Joseph grabbed a nearby slingshot and fired a rock straight into the animal's head. Amy grabbed the rat by the tail and threw it over the fire to singe off its wiry hair.

George watched in disgust.

Amy pulled the blackened carcass from the fire and began to scrape off the remaining hair. She wiped the body down, ensuring that it was clean, and then cut up the meat and organs into fine cubes. She added the meat to her soup, then stirred it well. "It'll be a few more minutes now," she said apologetically.

"You eat rats?" George asked, coughing his disapproval.

"You don't like rat?" Amy asked. "Why didn't you say something before I put it in the soup?"

George shook his head, not having a suitable answer.

"We were playing chess," Joseph said, intentionally changing the subject. "Do you play?"

George and Virginia had used to play chess often back when it was just the two of them. It was a decent enough way to pass the time, and it was engaging enough to take over for a while when the conversation went flat. Virginia and George hadn't played in a decade, but still just the thought of contemplating his various possible strategies sent images of Virginia's face to the forefront of his mind. "I'm not very good," he said with a shrug.

"I'm sure you're being modest," Joseph said. He returned to the chessboard and stared at the remaining pieces.

George found his bag close by, and he remembered the picture he had packed. "I'm looking for someone." He pulled the framed picture from a pocket and faced it toward Joseph and Amy. "She looks like this . . . only she might have deviant eyes now."

Joseph and Amy both got back up to look at the picture, confused even more about the eyes. Neither recognized the face, and they both shook their heads apologetically.

"She's very pretty," Amy said.

George gave her a pained smile, and then he tucked the photo back into his bag. "She's been missing since she left the hospital last week," he said, still trying to convince that small remaining slice of doubt inside him that she was still, indeed, alive.

"I hope you find her," Amy said, moving to stir the soup. She looked at the meat cooking in it and decided it could go a little longer.

Joseph and Amy returned to their game, and Joseph won after only two more turns.

"Cheater!" she joked.

"Is that a challenge for a rematch?" he asked.

George sat up straight, his heart suddenly pounding. "What day is it?" he asked.

Joseph and Amy each looked to the other for an answer, neither knowing.

George stared back for a moment, dumbfounded that the couple didn't know something as simple as the day.

"Are you okay?" Amy asked, alarmed by George's quick change in behavior.

"I have to get back! My kids! What if I already missed work?" George cried, panic rushing through him. He got to his feet and began to walk across the room, and then stopped and bent over, shaky and exhausted.

"I'm sure they'll understand," Joseph said. "You had a terrible fever."

"Yeah, that was my excuse last week," George muttered, feeling nauseous.

"Sit down and have some soup. You can eat around the rat meat," Amy said, going to the cauldron and giving it one last good stir. She ladled the dark soup into three bowls, making sure the men both got hearty servings.

George stirred his soup with his spoon, still not sure whether it smelled like something he would want to eat. Nothing but the rat meat was identifiable. "What else is in it?" he finally asked.

Amy shrugged, noting George's finicky palate. "A little of this, a little of that. It'll give you your strength back."

George watched Joseph and Amy eat the soup with no hesitations. Too hungry to pass on the meal, he tried a sip of the brown broth. It wasn't great, but it wasn't terrible, either. "Not bad," he said.

"Try it with a piece of meat," Joseph said.

Amy beamed.

Suddenly worrying over whether he was being a courteous guest, George tried the soup with a small cut of meat. He chewed slowly at first, and then gave Amy a satisfied smile. "Tastes like chicken."

"I've never tried chicken. I'm sure it's good, though, if it's anything like rat," Amy said, smiling back.

"It's better than rat," George said, and then chuckled at the sound of himself discussing the taste of rat.

Joseph went to the door and cracked it open. A few items of trash piled in from above as he peeked out, along with a bit of snow. He kicked them aside, notably unconcerned over their presence. "The storm still hasn't returned," he observed. "Looks like some of the snow is beginning to melt."

The stench of the trash piles came pouring in, and George realized that they were sitting inside one of the enormous piles. He took another look at his soup, and suddenly had to wonder where Amy had gotten all of her ingredients. His stomach going sour, he set down his bowl and pushed it away.

Joseph closed the door with a shiver. "It's still colder than hell out. Best to wait another day before making another attempt across to the market." He returned to his soup, noticing that George appeared to be finished. "Full already?"

George nodded. "You said there's a market on the other side? A deviant market?"

Joseph nodded. "I can take you there tomorrow as long as the weather holds up. We don't need the two of us getting snowed in on the way. Poor Amy would have one hell of a time dragging the both of us back to the fire," he said, turning and giving Amy a quick smile and wink.

George considered the offer, although a nagging thought in the back of his head told him that he was a fool not to be on his way home already, despite the persisting cold. Job abandonment was a serious offense, and the longer he waited, the more serious the repercussions would be when he did finally return. He wished he had at least some idea of what day it was.

He considered the repercussions that potentially existed if he did end his search for Virginia, knowing he might not be able summon up the energy or the courage to travel the district like this again. If he went back home, chances were he would return to the monotony of his job, lose himself trying to provide for his kids, and eventually give up on the idea that she was ever out there to begin with.

If he turned around now, everything he had gone through to get this far would all be for naught. Perhaps it was all for naught anyway, but he wouldn't be able to live with himself if he gave up without trying to find her.

George turned to Joseph and nodded his gratitude. "Thanks. I'll take you up on that."

# Chapter Twenty-Five

Shelley moved through the crowds of people assembling in the church's main lobby. Organ music played softly through loud speakers placed throughout the large area, and the acoustics created by the marble floor and vaulted ceilings caused the music to reverberate with an ethereal intensity. The lines to the registration consoles began to pick up and Shelley hurried outside, hoping no one important had seen her.

Shelly registered the family, solely to remove the threat of worship associates coming to their apartment that evening. They often came conveniently around dinnertime, wanting to know why the family had missed their services, never failing to invite themselves to whatever happened to be on the dinner table. It was best to keep the family on a low profile right now, given the circumstances.

The cold air hit her as she stepped outside. Sunlight broke through small gaps between the clouds, but it was not enough to take the chill away. The snow still stood several feet in most areas, and as a result, foot traffic was temporarily restricted to enclosed walkways. Luckily, most of the Sunday shuttles were running, some of them even on time, or services likely would have been canceled.

Shelley had no intention of finding her assigned seat and attending the morning sermon. She was there to find Charlotte, to see if her friends really could offer a better alternative to a life within the Mart Segregate. She only brought a single book bag with her, knowing she would stand out at church if she carried her enormous bags of clothes and notebooks with her through the lobby. Deep down, however, she left her other bags behind because she hoped her father might return before she had the chance to leave for good. She wanted to get Kurt's death off her chest. Perhaps she even wanted him to keep her from going through with her plan, to keep her from making such a grave mistake.

Running away was a serious matter. Part of her knew she was walking a thin line even by considering working outside both of the Segregates, and a nervous feeling in her gut told her she was too young to be leaving the safety of her childhood home. At the same time, she felt compelled to take a leap into the unknown, to be independent, to make her own rules, and to know real justice. Perhaps she was just looking for an excuse to escape the hell that had become her life. Either way, something needed to change.

Shelley entered the halls and slowly moved toward her old Sunday class building. She had a couple of hours to kill, so she took her time getting there. When she reached the appropriate building, she crouched down against the wall and wrapped her jacket tightly around her, hoping to protect the core of her body from the cool air blowing through the halls. The news associates wouldn't be out for a while, and not even a security associate stood outside the church's walls, the cold having driven everyone into the sermon room. All was silent beyond the rushes of cold air rolling through the halls and Shelley's shaky breaths.

She wondered how safe she was, at least a quarter of a mile away from the nearest security associate. If she had so easily registered for the morning and left, how many other people had done the same? The trick seemed simple enough to pull off, but she also just could have gotten lucky. Although she hadn't seen any security personnel guarding the entrance when she left, there had to be at least a few on the clock, watching the exits for potential deserters. Corporate seemed hell-bent on perfect attendance, and by the looks of the filled arena every Sunday, it was usually close.

Shelley looked down the hall in both directions, satisfying a sudden pang of apprehension that required she verify, without a doubt, that she was still alone. She wasn't sure why she was suddenly so anxious, and then she reminded herself that she had many life changes in store for her but still little idea of where she would be going. At least now she had some say in the direction she would be taking, whatever that would be, but when it all came down to it, her life was still just as uncertain as ever.

"Hey!" someone whispered.

She turned with a gasp, but saw no one. Her chest went uncomfortably tight as she listened vigilantly over the cold, unrelenting wind outside. She checked all of the nearby doors, surprised to find them unlocked. She slipped into her old classroom, relief hitting her as the door closed behind her and the room's central heating warmed her body.

She moved to the dry-erase board and read the lesson for the day. Not impressed, she wiped it clean and decided that a replacement lesson was in order. She found a permanent marker, tested it to make sure it was in good working order, and then proceeded to cover every inch of the white board with a dark, cryptic poem she had previously perfected in her head. A close reading of the poem would reveal many depressing truths to humankind and society, offering its readers a much more realistic approach to their day:

Compassion drains from the masses
   like blood from a pierced heart;
   a dark shroud blankets over them
   like black wool over their eyes.

The beast's tale shines as truth
   and the serpent eats the worm;
   hellfire crashes down as snow
   and they dance amidst the ashes.
      Where does the truth lie?

They come to worship death
   as the demon slowly sucks them dry;
   a choir of sirens takes the flock
   as they sing, "holy, holy, holy."

Black hearts wrapped in white silk
   that stain everything they touch;
   they merge into a gluttonous monster
   that slowly devours the world.
     Where does the truth lie?
     Where does the truth lie?

She wrote slowly and carefully, so that every word was straight and legible. She couldn't stand it when people wrote on a white board with that accidental slant to the top or to the bottom, failing miserably at keeping their words level with the frame. She would not be able to erase any potential mistakes, so she was determined that the finished piece come out as nothing short of pure art, both visually and in content. She kept her lines completely level, standing back every few seconds to make sure she had each stanza perfect. The marker she used was new, and it left behind lines and curves of flawless jet-black ink. She stood back and assessed her finished work. She smiled at the brilliance of her words, her perfect penmanship making them stand out on the board like a cleanly applied layer of paint to a newly whitewashed canvas.

Giddy, she decided she had time to publish some of her other work in the adjacent rooms. She carried the permanent marker with her, deciding already that she was going to stuff it in her bag when she was done to keep it as an honored trophy. It was a symbol of her freedom, her strike against conformity and oppression. Today, these classes would have a much-needed lesson in *grim reality*. Shelley felt that it was a subject all too often overlooked amid all of the

Leigh M. Lane

Bible quotes and news broadcasts. She felt the people deserved more variety in their lives. What better way to give it to them than with a set of gritty, plainspoken slice-of-real-life masterpieces honoring the nearly forgotten style of her favorite poets?

When the sermon let out, Shelley was back in the hall, contemplating going to one more classroom. She heard the sudden commotion of garbled voices and quick footsteps as the church doors opened and the people poured out into the distant halls. She ducked just to the inside of her building to wait for Charlotte, knowing that the crowds of students and class associates would be joining her soon enough.

A few people began to file in, some of them disappearing down the hall and in classrooms while others hurried up the stairs. No one took notice of Shelley, assuming she had just crossed the halls with the rest of them. She knew she needed to get out of there before anyone important saw what she had done, and she contemplated how much longer she would be able to wait before having to leave without seeing Charlotte. She was running out of time, and now wondered if perhaps this really wasn't the best time for her to be debuting her work to the masses.

"What the. . . ?" Shelley could hear a class associate exclaim upon entering one of the nearby rooms.

Charlotte entered the building, and Shelley yanked her aside. "We have to go!"

She hurried out and Charlotte raced after her. The two girls ran until neither could breathe, and Shelley made sure no one was watching them as she ducked down another hall to stop and catch her breath.

234

"What's going on?" Charlotte asked, her face tight with suspense.

"I changed the curriculum for the day," Shelley said with a wry smile. She giggled, thinking about how her poems were likely being received so far. Were the class associates already attempting to clean them off, their faces going red and their bodies beginning to sweat when the words refused to erase? Perhaps a handful of people read her work with great interest, glad to have something fresh and new to ponder? Maybe now she was more to her peers than simply the girl who was reclassified into the Mart Segregate.

Charlotte stared back, completely lost.

"I am now a published poet!" Shelley elaborated with a proud smile. "On the whiteboards of building C!"

"You did *not!*" Charlotte challenged with a surprised grin.

Shelley nodded. "All of my best work, now immortalized in permanent marker."

Charlotte squealed, unable to contain herself. "Please tell me you didn't sign them!"

Shelley shrugged, her smile bright with confidence. "Every one of them!"

"We've got to get out of here!" Charlotte giggled, her heart racing.

Shelley looked around, her excitement waning to a returned sense of anxiety and confinement. "Any ideas?"

"Maybe we should think on our way to the garage," Charlotte said, spotting a security associate moving across an adjacent hallway.

The girls hurried toward the shuttle garage, but reconsidered when they realized that a handful of security associates had been called out of class to guard the large area. They ducked behind the bend in the hallway. If anyone spotted them, both of them would probably be arrested. Shelley had committed at least four counts of Felony Corporate Crime: one count for presenting original literary material; another count for defacing church property; a third for blasphemy; and another for slandering Corporate. Shelley wondered why Charlotte seemed more excited than upset over being an accessory to such serious crimes, but she appreciated having a friend beside her while she scrambled to come up with a get-away plan.

The girls backtracked, turning down the next nearest side hall, finding that security associates were suddenly everywhere. As the crowds thinned from the halls and shuffled into the classrooms, their chances of being spotted grew. If they didn't get off church property soon, they would have no chance of escape.

Charlotte grabbed Shelley as they neared a crossroad in the hall. "There's a garbage chute at the end of the hall on the right."

Shelley turned down the hall, feeling uncertain. "Where's it lead?"

"Out of here, if you're lucky," Charlotte said with a shrug.

"You don't know?"

"I was class trash monitor back in the second grade. All I know is that's where all of the nearby classes dump their trash cans," Charlotte said. She ran ahead to the trash chute. "I always wanted to know where they led." She opened the large door to the chute, which slid down as it came open, much like a mailbox security door.

"You first," Shelley insisted.

Charlotte shook her head, holding the door open for Shelley. "You're the one who's in trouble, here! Better hurry up before someone sees you!"

Shelley looked down the long, dark chute. "What if I get stuck somewhere?"

"I'll be right behind you." Charlotte pushed Shelley toward the chute, and then coerced her into it headfirst. She closed the door, sending Shelley tumbling down, screaming.

CHARLOTTE OPENED the door, unable to see Shelley. "Hello?" she called.

There was no answer.

Having a last-second change of heart, Charlotte decided not to follow. "Hello?" she called again, a twinge of guilt moving through her. She spun around as a security associate came up behind her.

"Why aren't you in class?" the associate asked.

"Oh." Charlotte let go of the door, allowing it to snap shut. "I just had some trash I needed to toss."

"I need to see your I.D.," the associate said, holding out his hand.

Charlotte dug into her bag and found her identification card, and then handed it over to the security associate with an innocent smile.

The associate looked it over, decided that Charlotte was not the person he was searching for, and then handed the card back to her with a disappointed huff. "Get to class," he said.

Leigh M. Lane

"Yes, sir," Charlotte said, suppressing a giddy smile while she hurried past the man. She began toward her room, curious to see what mayhem had arisen as the result of Shelley's prank.

# Chapter Twenty-Six

Virginia waited all morning for Ray to arrive. It was only by luck that she'd found the hideout, after having wandered the district all day, completely lost. As she drifted through the different areas, looking for a shuttle line she recognized, she was surprised to see how differently society treated her while she wore her Corporate disguise. How strange that the coat she wore could offer her so much respect, and how completely opposite her treatment would surely be if she were to remove her sunglasses and just one person got a good glimpse of her eyes. Men opened doors for her; managers offered her their shuttle seats. She wondered how many laws she broke by playing the part and accepting their kind gestures, but then decided that she didn't really care. After everything she had gone through, she deserved a bit of pampering.

When she finally found her way, moving through the piles of snow left by yesterday's heavy storm, she became even more grateful for the expensive clothing. She pushed her way through the slushy trails in the field, the heavy boots protecting her feet from the cold. She kept her hands in the coat's deep pockets, the thick pelts guarding her from the frozen air.

Ray's people ambushed her when she reached the cave, intent on mugging and killing her. Several men rushed her, and it wasn't until they dragged her, kicking and screaming, into the main room and saw her eyes that they realized she wasn't just a lost Corporate. Virginia brushed herself off and took some time to calm down, only to find that Ray had been called to another location for the weekend. Isaac offered her a spare bed, but Virginia insisted upon spending the night in one of the office chairs, waiting where she was until Ray returned in the morning.

She wore Mrs. Conrad's expensive coat and accessories throughout the night, despite the well-heated room, afraid that it might disappear forever if she were to take it off. She woke in a heavy sweat, but still she refused to give up even the boots or hat, determined that she would have the means to brave the cold again if need be.

The morning slowly moved into afternoon, and Virginia slipped outside to check on the weather. The snow was melting quickly, although the temperature had risen only slightly since yesterday. Ray would be back any time, now, according to the men guarding the place, although they had been insisting upon his arrival for hours. Virginia felt like she was wasting time just sitting there, waiting, while Corporate actively planned their demise.

Ray finally arrived in the late afternoon,

accompanied by several other people Virginia did not recognize.

Virginia hurried up to Ray and followed him into the main cave. "I need to talk to you."

Ray seemed surprised to see Virginia, and even more surprised at her attire. "Virginia, right?"

Virginia nodded. "I really need to talk to you."

Ray sat down at his desk, logging onto his computer. He turned to one of his men. "I want a full report every hour."

The man nodded, and then he and the others disappeared down a rocky hall.

Ray took a deep breath and turned to Virginia. "I'm sorry, my dear, but aren't you supposed to be at the Conrads' estate?"

"There was an incident," Virginia said, not wanting to rehash all of the horrible details. "I found some interesting information on their computer, though—"

"We already received the information from one of my other men," Ray said gruffly, but then smiled and patted her on the shoulder. "But good job. At least I know whose side you're on."

Virginia frowned, taken aback. "What do you mean by that?"

Ray gave his most sincere face, and he answered directly and without hesitation. "It would only be natural for you to have some enduring loyalties to your old life. I'm actually quite impressed with your development. Perhaps your brain actually did catch up with your eyes."

Virginia wiped the sweat from the side of her face and neck, no longer able to handle the heavy layers of fur. She took off the hat and unbuttoned her coat. With another thought, she kicked off the boots, sighing with great relief as her body breathed for the first time in two days.

Ray inputted several commands with a few clicks of the mouse, his attention quickly returning to his computer. He watched her in the reflection of this monitor as he worked. "I assume that is Mrs. Conrad's coat you're wearing?"

"How else was I going to get back here through the snow?"

"May I ask if you know whether Mrs. Conrad is still alive?" Ray asked.

"Why do you ask?"

Ray picked up his hand-held computer and began inputting commands. "Her last login was quite disturbing," he said as he turned to face Virginia. "You said there was an incident?"

Virginia took a deep breath, and then proceeded to explain the series of events to the best of her ability. Ray stared back for a moment, taking in the story, and then he began to punch in a few new commands on his hand-held computer.

"But you would say Mrs. Conrad is probably still alive?" he asked.

"I locked her in the basement."

Ray entered a command for one of his most seasoned men to investigate the Conrad estate before he set the hand-held into its computer port. He synchronized the databases, sending his commands to the other headquarters.

Ray and Isaac had come up with an immediate counterattack to Corporate's development of HD-1a, as well as Mrs. Conrad's allegation that deviants had killed her husband. Isaac had his laboratory staff working at all four locations to produce enough Blue Dust to infect the entire quadroplex. Meanwhile, Ray had assassins hunting down every Corporate their intelligence could track, silently taking them down, one by one, as they left from their fortress-like estates.

"I'm still looking for volunteers for our next big project," Ray said. "Can I count on your help?"

Virginia nodded.

"You look like you could use a hot bath." Ray pointed to a narrow tunnel on his right. "I've got a tub in my sleeping quarters. You can get cleaned up in there, scrub your clothes." He immediately shifted his attention back to his work, letting her know that their conversation was over.

"Thanks," Virginia said, moving to the dark cave. "Where's the light?" she asked, hesitant to go any further.

"Motion activated," he said, annoyed.

Virginia slipped through the narrow tunnel, feeling her way to the adjoining cave. As Ray promised, an overhead light flickered on as soon as she entered the large room.

There was a king-sized bed on one side, two dressers, and a bathtub with hot running water. Virginia waited to make sure no one followed behind her, and then she filled the tub and removed her sweaty clothes. The hot bath was relaxing, and it felt good to rinse off the sticky layer of sweat her body had accumulated over the past couple of days. Still, she washed and got out as quickly as she could, wrapping herself in Ray's thick bathrobe. She scrubbed her clothes in the warm, soapy water, and then hung them to dry along the side of the tub.

Holding the robe close to her body, Virginia padded barefoot through the tunnel, finding Ray right where she had left him. Beside him, however, there was now an untouched tray of fruit and sandwiches.

"Lunch?" Ray asked as Virginia slowly entered the cave.

Virginia hurried to the food, taking a small helping of all that was offered.

Ray picked up a peanut butter sandwich and leisurely nibbled at it. "Slow down. You'll give yourself indigestion." He confirmed that all of his logistics were set, and then flipped off the computer monitor. "I see you found something clean to change into."

Virginia blushed, clasping the fabric with one hand to keep her chest and legs from showing through. "I couldn't find anything else."

Unable to eat any more, Virginia found a chair and curled up beneath the robe. She watched Ray slowly finish his sandwich, the silence killing her. "I know why you developed HD-1, the Blue Dust, or whatever you want to call it," she finally said. "I'm not sorry this happened to me. Not anymore, anyway. I've seen so much . . . and I'm glad to know what I now know."

"I'm glad to hear that," Ray said, visibly contemplating all that remained available on the food tray. He picked up a nectarine and took a large, juicy bite. He chewed slowly, savoring the sweet fruit. "We stole a whole shipment of these from Corporate growers in this district. We're selling them at the deviant market for ten cents on the dollar." He gave Virginia a dire look. "Scurvy is a big problem in the shantytowns."

Virginia looked down, feeling as though she needed to apologize for all of the suffering deviants had endured throughout the years. She had to apologize for humanity, and for all the years she took her freedom and her rights as a human being for granted. "I'm sorry," she finally said aloud.

"Beg pardon?" Ray asked, finishing his nectarine, licking the juice from his fingers.

"I'm sorry that humanity let you all down so miserably," Virginia said, her throat knotting up.

"Humanity let you down too, if I remember correctly," he quickly replied, setting the nectarine pit aside.

Virginia nodded, and she covered her face with embarrassment as she began to cry.

"You've lost a lot, my dear," Ray continued, getting up and wiping off his hands. He went over to her and put a hand on her shoulder. "I can tell you're a strong woman. You'll survive this."

Virginia looked up, feeling a sense of calm from his reassuring face. He wiped away her tears, and she closed her eyes as his hand gently caressed her face. His hands smelled faintly of nectarine, the sweet scent soothing and inviting.

"I'm sorry," she said once more, another wave of tears coming as her mind drifted to thoughts of her estranged husband and kids.

"It's time now to think of the future," Ray said, wiping away her new tears. "Dwelling on the past will only hold you back."

She nodded.

"Oh, I almost forgot." He fished her wedding band from a drawer. "No harm in you wearing it now."

She held it for a moment, put it on her left ring finger only to move it immediately to her right. She looked at it, reveled in the feel of it on her finger, and then pulled it off with a light cry. "For the future," she said as she dropped the gold ring into the palm of Ray's hand and closed it into a tight fist.

Ray's eyes met hers, and he gave her a quick nod of gratitude. "A generous donation."

He wiped her face once more, the smell of nectarines brushing over her cheeks, and then he softly kissed her anxious lips.

She turned away. "I'm sorry . . . I can't."

He watched her, his face wrought with desire and confusion as she turned back and their eyes met again. She wiped the tears from her face and new ones immediately took their place.

He clasped the wedding band tightly in his hand, then disappeared alone down the dark cave.

# Chapter Twenty-Seven

George followed Joseph through the wet, smelly trails leading to the edge of town. Joseph had a bag of items with him, cleaned up bits of trash with which he could barter at the market for necessities. The two chatted casually while they went. Joseph made the trip roughly once a week, picking up as many food staples and toiletries as his bag of recycled trash could buy. Amy generally stayed behind to guard their home from potential invaders, and as a result, the nearly two-mile walk was usually lonely. Sometimes, he would find more items along the way to add to his bag, although stopping to search through the distant piles always inevitably tacked even more time onto his already lengthy trip. Every once in a while, he would bump into a neighbor on his way, but usually he didn't see another soul until he neared the market.

George continuously gagged, the melting snow bringing out the worst of the pungent, decomposing stench all around them. He looked around, his stomach nauseated even further by the inescapable

Leigh M. Lane

sight of soggy trash and rust-colored puddles of garbage water. He noticed that Joseph didn't seem bothered at all by it or the endless mountains of trash, and he assumed that the poor man's olfactory system had burned out long ago from living amongst that rotten, putrid smell for so many years.

"I hope the weather holds," Joseph said, wary of the lingering clouds.

"It just seems to get worse every year," George said, not offering a direct response to Joseph's comment, but keeping the small-talk going just the same.

"You're not kidding." Joseph shifted his bag from one shoulder to the other, the weight of it beginning to pull uncomfortably against his back. "I hope the cold weather doesn't affect today's market. That last flash-blizzard caught a lot of people off-guard," he added, his tone of voice offering a genuine level of concern.

George slowed his pace as the piles of trash on his left gave way to an immense automobile graveyard. Old metal frames, engines, and compacted cubes sat piled amongst rusty remnants of the Old World's most popular form of transportation. George remembered automobiles. He had never driven one, but he had ridden in many of them up until his early teens. They became obsolete even before fossil fuels became scarce, phased out in a last ditch effort to reverse the effects of global warming. Of course, the effort came far too late, and the Big Climate Change happened anyway.

George marveled at the piles of twisted metal, reminiscing back to the all but completely forgotten days of road trips, family vacations, and regular visits with relatives. The world had been a far different place for almost as long as he could remember, and sometimes he forgot how much life really had changed through the years. He stopped for a moment, his breath still, as he and Joseph came upon the remains of a large, commercial airliner.

Joseph stopped with George, assuming the older man had never before seen a vehicle so large. "It's called an aero-jet. They say people used to get these heavy behemoths up in the air, somehow, and keep them there long enough to fly anywhere across the globe. It seems impossible, I know, but—"

"I remember airplanes," George gently interrupted.

Joseph turned to George, surprised. "You do?"

George took one last good look at the dead mechanical structures at his side then continued down the trail. It was strange how familiar, yet so equally foreign, the vehicles were. He never had the opportunity to fly before all of the commercial airlines shut down, but he remembered watching planes cross the sky when he was very young. Sometimes he would wonder if those memories were no more than petty childhood imaginings: spectral flying machines that disappeared from the skies once Santa Claus and the Easter Bunny fell into their rightful ranks of childhood fantasy. With everything he just saw, however, he knew that they all had to have been real . . . every single one of them.

Once upon a time.

George wondered if he looked hard enough, or dug deep enough through the endless piles of trash, perhaps he'd find that God was buried somewhere out there as well.

The stench compounded itself once more as the cars and airplanes disappeared and became replaced by more towering piles of rotting food containers, discarded treasures, and dirty diapers. Another young deviant emerged from a nearby pile, carrying his own bag of findings for the market.

Joseph nodded at the other deviant in a friendly greeting.

The deviant nodded back at Joseph, and then saw George's brown eyes. He ducked his head low and silently hurried down the trail, gaining considerable distance between them in a mere ten of fifteen seconds.

"What was that all about?" George asked.

"He had a rough experience with a human once. Don't take it personally," Joseph said.

"You know that guy?" George asked, watching the frightened young man disappear into the distance up ahead.

Joseph shrugged. "I should—he's one of my neighbors."

"I hate my neighbors," George said.

Joseph looked at George, surprised. "They must be pretty rotten people."

George thought about it for a moment, and then shook his head. "No, not really."

Joseph let the issue drop, redirecting George's attention to a plateau that became visible as they came to the top of a short hill. "We're not far now," he said, pointing to the flat, untended expanse of land up ahead.

To the right, deviant workers manned giant rail

carts filled with trash. They seemed to be bringing it in from a distant location, and then shoveling it into the tall piles George and Joseph now passed the last of. The workers took turns looking up from their task, all of them recognizing Joseph, each reacting in various ways to George's presence.

George dug into his bag and pulled out a picture of Virginia. He held it up for the workers to see. "Have any of you seen my wife?"

Most of the men took a good look, but none seemed to recognize her face. George put away the photo with a tired sigh, and he and Joseph moved on.

"The market is just ahead," Joseph said as they continued down the path and entered the five-foot-tall field of wild grass. Small patches of snow still blanketed the field, and the path was slick with sheets of ice.

A ninety-degree fork appeared in the path, and Joseph and George veered to the left. The busy sound of bartering and networking slowly became audible, and then seemingly out of nowhere there was an enormous clearing filled with hundreds of deviants and their wares.

There were no booths or kiosks, but a few inventive people had set up small tables, brought folding chairs, or set up makeshift umbrellas. Some went from person to person, trading wherever they could. There were a few fruit stands, one person selling rats, a clothing peddler, a man who'd somehow obtained commercially packaged bags of rice, and another walking around with a bag full of batteries. George figured the inventory here likely changed by the week, but those who had the means could go home with a decent variety of household staples.

"Good luck finding your wife," Joseph said.

George nodded. "Thanks." He looked around, noticing several suspicious eyes watching him.

The two shook, and then Joseph disappeared into the crowd of browsers and traders.

George slowly moved through the crowd, flashing Virginia's picture in all directions. Most of the people there seemed confused to see a lone human walking through their market, and a few strong young men followed him to ensure he was not up to any foul play.

George tried to look as non-threatening as possible, holding Virginia's picture between him and his onlookers.

"Whatcha got there?" a young man sitting with a cage of rats asked, taking notice of George and his numerous onlookers.

George walked up to the man, keeping the picture up in front of him. "I'm looking for this woman."

"Never seen her. Would you like to buy a rat?" the man replied.

George shook his head, turning away.

The overlooking group drew closer as Ray's associate, Mary, who happened to be shopping at the time, slowly approached George to get a closer look at Virginia's picture. She nodded with absolute certainty. "I've seen her."

George grabbed the young woman's arm. "You have to tell me where she is!"

There was suddenly a group of silent, staring deviants surrounding them. George froze, realizing that his stance probably appeared threatening to those nearby, and he let go of Mary's arm, backing off a few steps with his hands in the air. "I'm sorry."

Mary eyed the crowd, then turned back to George. "Why do you want to find her?"

"She's my wife," George said, fighting to hold onto his composure. "I just want to take her home."

"And you're searching for her here why?"

He hesitated, swallowing hard. "Because I think she might be . . . like you."

Mary nodded, her face going soft and compassionate. "I can have someone track her down for you. Where are you staying?"

George shrugged. "Can't you just take me to her?"

"Unfortunately, I can't."

George shook his head, defeated. "She doesn't want to see me?"

"I don't have the authority to take you where she is," Mary said.

"Can you take me to someone who does?" The weight of a hundred eyes watching him in his agony felt like enough to make him nearly collapse. He looked down, dizzy with apprehension.

Mary thought for a moment. "I can't make you any promises, but let me see what I can do. Meet me here later, after dusk?"

George nodded anxiously, barely able to breathe. "I'll be here."

Mary nodded and then continued with her shopping. The crowd slowly resumed its regular business, haggling and bartering despite George's presence.

She turned back, and their eyes met one last time

before she disappeared into the thin crowd.

He stood where he was, a standing vigil, vowing not to move again until he had Virginia in his arms.

# Chapter Twenty-Eight

Shelley scrambled in an attempt to climb out of the giant trash bin. She was waist-deep in garbage, which luckily was composed mostly of discarded scrap paper and classroom supplies. She cringed and gagged when her hand went into a wad of discarded chewing gum, however, and she wiped it clean as well as she could against the metal side of the bin.

The bin seemed to be rolling on an electronic track, moving at a slow but steady pace deeper and deeper into unknown territory. Shelley couldn't see much, given how high the sides of the bin were, but she could see parts of some of the taller buildings and shuttle tracks she passed. She didn't recognize any of the buildings, and she had no idea what direction she was going. It felt like she had been moving for hours, although she had no way of gauging how long she actually had been in there.

The trash chute back at the church grounds had sent her gracelessly flailing down into the bin, which seemed to move on a timer. It was evident that no one staffed the immediate area, because Shelley screamed and cried for help until her throat went raw and no one seemed to hear her. If there were any people nearby, they certainly did not make themselves known.

The bin was filled with too many flimsy materials for Shelley to be able to pile them up and climb, although she did make several attempts before she realized the futility in it. She tried springing up against the sides, scaling the smooth walls, and even knocking the entire unit off its track, but every attempt she made to escape ended in failure. She eventually gave up, exhausted and emotionally spent, and fell back against the trash to watch the sky slowly move over her.

A thick cloud overhead held an uncanny likeness to Kurt's face, and Shelley stared at it in disbelief. Of all the shapes a cloud could take, the one right overhead had to look like her dead brother. Slowly, the face changed as the cloud drifted in the light breeze. The image grew angry. A heavy gust of wind whipped by overhead, and Shelley could have sworn that she heard Kurt's furious voice: "You!"

Shelley cried out, cringing and covering her face. "You're not Kurt!"

She waited for the voice to return, but it did not. The wind died down, and the only sound that remained was the creak of the trash bin wheels slowly rolling along the rails. She peeked up at the sky, sighing with relief as she saw that the face in the cloud had dissipated into an indistinguishable mass of random shapes.

She caught a whiff of something foul, and then

took a few deep breaths in attempt to place the smell. She looked in all directions, and she noticed that there were no more visible buildings. The smell grew stronger, and as the bin continued along its track, it occurred to Shelley that she was moving along the outskirts of the local dump.

Shelly quietly listened, staying completely still, as the bin suddenly jerked to a halt. All was silent for a moment, and then Shelley heard a handful of voices coming from outside.

"Hello?" Shelley called.

"There's someone in that one!" a young male voice cried out.

"Hello?" Shelley yelled, hitting the side of the bin.

"Lean against the wall, toward my voice!" the young man called back.

"Okay!" Shelley leaned against the wall, tightly shutting her eyes. There was a loud click, and then the bin slammed to its side. The piles of trash spilled over her and onto the ground, and Shelly scrambled out of the bin. She held onto the icy ground for a moment, her head spinning.

"Are you okay?" a young man asked.

Shelly looked up, gasping at the sight of the small deviant group. They all wore hard hats and carried shovels. She saw the shovels and considered the damage they could do if the men decided to attack her, and she screamed. She pulled herself to her feet, dizzy and shaking, and grabbed her bag. Two men tried to assist her, and she took a pathetic swing at them both with a terrified growl. The men all quickly backed off, grumbling at her detestable manners.

She staggered back, running into a pile of trash

just recently stacked, and then she scrambled into the path and ran off. The men laughed as she hurried away, their voices carrying past the mountains of trash as she quickly moved to put them behind her. She tried to keep from crying, but she felt her will deteriorating. Finding herself suddenly on the deviant side of town, possibly even in a neighboring district with no idea how to get home, she found herself dizzy with fear. She shook profusely, unsure what to do or where to go.

She could not see any signs of civilization anywhere. Knowing she could run into more deviants at any time, she stayed along the cusp of the dump, searching through the trash piles for a suitable weapon. She hoped to find an old hammer or a steel pipe, but she decided to settle for the time being on a piece of cinder block. She put the chunk of cement in her bag, and then swung it around a few times to get a feel for her new weapon. Satisfied, she continued forward with the dump to her left and nothing but overgrown, empty fields on her right.

The sun peeked through the clouds, and Shelley could feel its warmth against her cheeks despite the chill that persisted in the air. She did her best to ignore the growl hitting her stomach. Thirst soon compounded her hunger, and she knew one of the two would have to be satiated soon.

She stopped to search for a clean patch of snow in the field when she heard a rustling nearby in the tall grass. Certain that one of the young men she passed at the trash had followed her, she went vigilant and still. She considered what terrible deeds he had planned in that sick, deviant mind of his, and knew that it was up to her to put him in his place. She readied her bag and held her breath as the rustling drew closer. She saw two deviant eyes emerge from the grass, and a sudden impulse drove her to swing her bag with all that she had. The cinder block met the back of the young man's head, and he collapsed with a surprised cry.

Shelley's hands shook violently while she watched the blood seep onto the snow-spattered ground, and she knew right away that she had killed him. At a closer glance, she realized that the young deviant couldn't have been much older than she was, and he had been completely unarmed. Distraught and exhilarated, Shelley dragged the body back into the cover of the tall grass. She stared at it for a moment, watching its glassy blue eyes stare aimlessly up toward the heavens.

"This one's one for my mom," she said, her throat growing tight. She spat on the body, and then hurried back to the path. She began to cry again, screaming out her frustration as she forced away the immense guilt that filled her over what she had just done. She saw the blood on her bag, and her entire body froze. She felt dizzy, and then she found herself on her knees. She continued to stare at the blood for a moment, sobbing, when suddenly she realized that she was laughing.

She picked herself up and continued down the path, pulling her bag back up over her shoulder. She looked across the field, wondering how many more deviants were hiding in the overgrowth. She picked a random spot and entered the field, pushing aside tall grass and slushy masses of snow. She walked aimlessly through the grass for some time, and then she came upon a small clearing that had a tiny, three-walled shack and a recently extinguished fire pit. A clean pot and pan sat beside the smoking pit, and a stash of rice and canned fruits sat just inside the shack. There were blankets on the dusty ground, and a pile of clothing in the far corner. A pail of clean water stood next to a plastic bin of mismatched dishes and silverware, and strips of dried meat hung from a hook on the ceiling.

Listening carefully for the sounds of others approaching, Shelly hastily searched through the plastic bin, finding a large, well-sharpened knife worth adding to her bag. She helped herself to the dried meat, gazing at the drab plywood walls and considering leaving her mark.

Finding her permanent marker, she went to the flimsy wall and began to write. She came up with a simple poem off the top of her head, slowly chewing on the meat as she carefully yet quickly placed her words:

Thanks for the food,
sorry to be so rude,
I hope you rot in hell.

Finishing a handful of meat, she signed the wall in large, fancy letters. She drank as much water as her stomach would allow, and then moved to look through the small selection of canned fruits.

She threw three cans of peaches into her bag and pilfered the rest of the dried meat before stepping out of the shack. She opened one of the peach cans, eating the sweet fruit with her dirty hands. She glanced out over the field, contemplating her next move, when she spotted a small bug moving across the ground in front of her. She squashed it with a quick stomp of her foot.

Tossing the used fruit can to the ground, she chose a random direction and began to walk.

# Chapter Twenty-Nine

Virginia sat near Ray, still clad in his robe, as she watched him search his updated files for a new job to assign her. The robe was warm enough, but she felt only half-clad wearing it. She was still waiting for a layer or two of her new clothes to dry out.

"Would you like to work on a field job this time?" Ray asked.

Virginia shrugged. "What would I do?"

"Well, wearing that fancy coat of yours, you'd have no problem handing out free samples at the district Food-Mart," Ray said, smiling at the prospect.

"Free samples of what?" Virginia asked.

"Does it matter?"

"People will just end up going to the hospital and disappearing," she said, her voice flat. "I don't want to be responsible for anyone else going through that."

"I can assure that won't be happening for much longer."

Virginia shook her head, hoping he might elaborate. When he said nothing, she finally asked, needing to confirm her suspicion: "You're planning a mass release?"

"We have no choice. We have to do this now, before Corporate has enough HD-1a to do the same," Ray said, the resolve clear in his unwavering voice. "Our most recent intelligence suggests a Corporate strike could occur as early as by the end of the week. We have to act before they do."

He explained to Virginia that he had assigned workers to seed hospital and shuttle garage air ducts, some to infect school hallways, and others working the outskirts of all the tunnels, handing HD-1-tainted cards and jewelry to anyone with non-deviant eyes.

Virginia glanced at the computer screen, surprised at how vast and organized his operation actually was. How one man could pull together such complicated logistics with just that little hand-held computer and a synch port was beyond her. It seemed he truly did have the means to succeed in pulling off the quadroplex-wide endeavor. From what she had seen on the Corporate Internet, however, the deviant's attempt really did need to be made either immediately or not at all.

"Are you in or out? I need to update my computers," Ray said, finishing up with the rest of the assignments.

"I'm in," Virginia said, although she still was not exactly sure how dirty she wanted to get her hands.

"Are you positive?" he asked, sensing the hesitation in her voice. "I can put you on a job that starts tomorrow."

"Positive," Virginia said, still trying to convince herself. "I'm going to go check on my clothes."

She quietly walked out, into Ray's room, going to the side of the tub and feeling the different articles for dampness. She decided to wait for them to finish drying in the solitude of the quiet cave, away from Ray, his computers, and his men. She needed to take a breather, if only for a short while, to calm her nerves and find the strength to continue.

"Hello? Are you decent?" Mary called from the other side of the tunnel.

Virginia turned, making sure the robe fully covered her. "Yes."

Mary hurried in. "Virginia?"

"Yes?"

Mary hesitated for a moment, then said, "Your husband is looking for you. I ran into him today at the market."

Virginia felt her body go weak, and for a moment, she thought she might pass out. Dizzy and distraught, she began to cry. "Is he still there?"

"He said he would meet you there this evening," Mary said.

"George is *looking* for me?" Virginia cried, still in shock over the news.

Mary nodded. "I can take you to him."

"You can't go back to your old life," Ray said, having listened in on the women and decided it was finally time to step in. He held a glitter-covered business card up between two fingers. "You can, however, bring your family into the new." He walked up to Virginia and offered it to her.

Virginia stared at the card, afraid to touch it.

"The dust doesn't do anything to us," Ray said, shifting the card to his other hand and licking a layer of blue glitter from one of his fingers. He held it out again, and Virginia hesitantly took it into her shaky hand.

"It's completely safe?" Virginia asked.

"Completely." Ray gathered Virginia's half-dried clothes and dropped them in her arms. "Mary will escort you." He motioned to Mary, moving toward the tunnel.

Mary nodded then followed Ray out to his office.

Virginia quickly put on her clothes, ignoring the large wet spots. She slipped on her boots, and then grabbed her hat and jacket on her way to the tunnel, tucking the business card in one of the pockets. She moved quietly as she neared the cave mouth, realizing that Ray and Mary were whispering.

"I just want you to keep an eye on her for me," Ray said. "Make sure there aren't any last-minute changes of heart."

"Does that mean I'm on the clock?"

Ray chuckled lightly. "Of course."

Virginia quietly entered the cave, and Ray and Mary both went silent. Virginia gave them both a strained smile, feigning ignorance of their brief exchange. She brushed at the wet spots in her clothes, pretending to be distracted.

Ray and Mary exchanged a quick glance.

"I'm sorry, was I interrupting something?" she asked.

Ray smiled. "Nothing at all."

"Ready?" Mary asked her, smiling and taking a deep breath.

Virginia nodded.

Ray gave Virginia a friendly pat on the back.

"You're doing the right thing."

Virginia nodded again. Without another word, she followed Mary out through the cave and began down the hidden trail that led to the market.

# Chapter Thirty

George only left his spot once, and only long enough to relieve himself nearby in a patch of tall bushes. Joseph had long gone, content with the bag of rice, fresh razor, and pound of dried fruit he ended up with by his final trade. The hours went by slowly, but the afternoon eventually lapsed into evening. The sun set, and twilight soon turned to dark. The temperature dropped back below freezing, and George watched as the people, one by one, packed up their wares and the crowds thinned to just a handful of stragglers. He held his jacket tightly around him, wrapping his scarf over his nose and mouth.

He worked to look calm and controlled, feeling increasingly threatened the darker and the more desolate the market became. He noticed that a few younger males who had been loitering and goofing around for hours had been taking turns looking over at him for some time. He made sure to establish eye contact whenever he could, to let the young deviants know that he was aware of them and not intimidated by their presence.

The group slowly made their way closer, wary of the trespassing human. One of them built up the courage to face George, and he stood in front of him with a malevolent sneer. "Do you have something to trade?"

George stared down the young man, ignoring an intense urge to look away. "I'm just waiting for someone."

"You picked an interesting place to meet," the deviant said, holding his fix just as intently on George's unwavering eyes.

George gave a light shrug. "You could say that."

The deviant turned back to his friends, who inched closer behind him. "I think we should make a trade," he said.

George felt himself go tense. "I don't have anything to trade."

"That jacket looks warm," the deviant said, turning back once more to flash a smile to his friends.

George continued to stare down the young man. "I'm not trading my jacket."

"No?" The deviant grabbed George by his backpack, sending him to the ground. He kicked George in the stomach. "You and your expensive clothes! Did you come here just to flaunt what you have? Don't you have anything better to do with your time, rich man?" he asked.

George balled up on the ground, struggling to regain the wind that had been kicked out of him. He covered his head and face, should the deviant throw another kick his way.

"What is your problem?" Mary yelled from the

edge of the field.

The young men froze and turned to Mary, and then backed away from George.

"Get the hell out of here!" Mary yelled. "Ray has immediate assignments for all of you!"

The young men silently disappeared down the path.

Virginia came up behind Mary, wearing dark glasses. George assumed she feared his potential reaction to her eyes, and she visibly shook with apprehension. The sunglasses left her virtually blind in the dark, however, and she didn't even notice George until she heard his voice.

"Virginia?" George called out to her as he caught his breath.

Virginia stumbled across the clearing, peeking below her glasses as she quickened her pace. "George!"

They came together in a tight embrace, and then kissed passionately. They both cried, holding on as though they might lose one another once more if one of them were to let go. The rest of the world seemed to fall out of existence for the moment.

"How did you know I was still alive?" Virginia asked.

"I just knew," George said. He went to remove her sunglasses, and she grabbed his hand. "Let me see," he said.

Her hand slowly eased up, and he slipped the sunglasses from her face. She looked up at him, anxiously holding her breath.

"I missed you," George said, looking into her eyes. "Let's go home."

Virginia glanced over at Mary, who silently shook her head at her.

"I can't go back," Virginia said. "Not yet, anyway."

"We'll find a way to make it work!" George said, his voice going desperate.

Virginia took a deep breath. "The world is changing. Half of the quadroplex will be infected with HD-1 by the end of tomorrow. The deviant underground is in the middle of a strike to overturn Corporate. The world as we know it is at an end."

George shook his head. "What are you talking about?"

Virginia pulled the business card from her pocket, and George jumped back when he saw the glitter dropping from it.

"What are you doing?" George asked, his voice shaking. He stared at the card, holding a comfortable distance between them.

"I want you and the kids to come with me. We can start over," Virginia said, extending the card to George.

"Keep that thing away from me!" he cried.

Virginia pulled back, unsure what to do next.

George noticed that Virginia's hands were bare. "Where's your wedding ring?"

Virginia looked down at her ring finger, and then shook her head. "I lost it."

Mary hurried impatiently up to Virginia. She glared over at George. "You should come with us."

"I'm taking my wife home with me," George said firmly. "Please excuse us."

"I don't have time for this," Mary mumbled as she

attempted to snatch the business card from Virginia's hand.

Virginia resisted her, and the two women went to the ground as Mary swept her legs. George jumped back, his eyes staying on the glittery card, as the two women fought over it. After only a moment, however, Mary let her go.

Virginia jumped to her feet. "Go home! I'll find you!" she yelled to George, then ran off with the card, a trail of glitter shimmering behind her in the cloud-dampened moonlight.

Mary looked at her hand, noticing the small amount of Blue Dust she had been able to pull off the card. She lunged at George as he attempted to pass her, smacking him in the face with her infected hand.

George stared at the woman for a moment, stunned.

Mary held up her hand, showing him the remnants of glitter that still stuck to her fingers. "It's for the best. Trust me," she said.

George wiped at his face, finding traces of glitter on his fingers. "Why?"

"You'll thank me later."

George cried out, swinging at Mary with an angry right hook. He hit her squarely in the temple, and she fell to the ground, going quiet and still.

George kept his distance despite the fact that she stayed down. He felt bad that he had hit the woman, but he agonized over the fact that he hadn't been quick enough to keep her from hitting him first. He looked around, seeing no one else around, and then turned to the trail to find his wife. "Virginia!" he yelled as loudly as he could.

VIRGINIA HEARD George's call, but she continued along the trail. She sobbed uncontrollably, running as quickly as her legs could take her. She had no idea where she was going, but she figured that it really didn't matter at this point.

"Virginia!" George called again from the distance.

Virginia continued down the path, falling to the ground with a loud cry as she ran straight into Shelley.

Shelley went down with her, and she scrambled to her feet. "What the hell is your—" Shelley fell silent when she recognized Virginia's face. Shelly began to shake, eyeing the glittery business card in Virginia's hand and the expensive Corporate coat now soiled with mud.

Virginia gasped, and then took a strained breath. "My baby?" Tears streamed down her cheeks and a relieved smile fell across her face. "I thought I'd never see you again!" she cried. "God, what did you do to your eye?" She got to her feet, dropping the business card, losing herself in the moment and forgetting the glitter that remained on her fingers.

Shelley backed away from her. Her throat knotted up so tightly she feared she might stop breathing. "You're dead!" she gasped.

"They lied," Virginia said, carefully matching Shelley's steps, desperate for Shelley to know the truth.

Shelley quickly dug into her bag and pulled out the knife. She held it up, pointing it at Virginia. "You're lying!" She forced in another heart-wrenching gasp, crying out, fighting to breathe. Tears streamed down her confused, horrified face. "Stop haunting me!"

"It's me," Virginia cried. She held her hands up in the air. "Put down the knife, sweetie!"

They made eye contact, but they only held it for a moment. Shelley gave her a sideways glance, visibly disgusted by the sight of her deviant-blue eyes.

"Tell me who sent you," Shelley demanded, waving the knife wildly in front of her, prompting Virginia to flinch back. "Tell me where you came from!"

"I got lost! You have to believe me!"

"Imposter!" Shelley screamed. "My mother's *dead*!"

"I'm right here!"

"No!" Shelley fell to her knees and covered her ears with her hands. Her body shook violently, then she shrieked in terror as Virginia tried to close the gap between them.

"Virginia!" George called from somewhere in the distance.

"George!" Virginia called back. She quickly turned back to Shelley, startled by the blank expression that had taken over her daughter's face. "Shelley, you need to listen to me," she said as calmly as she could.

"I don't think so," Shelley said, her voice suddenly equally as calm.

A shiver ran down Virginia's spine while she searched the cold eyes staring back at her for some hint of the daughter she had left behind. She cleared her tight throat. "I'm still me."

Shelley glanced down at Virginia's hands, then stared back up into her pale eyes. "I don't know you!"

"How can you say that?" Virginia cried aloud, her

grief growing worse than any physical pain she'd ever encountered.

Shelly scurried to her feet as Virginia, desperate to reassure the girl, rushed up to her. She tried to push the knife out of the way and embrace her frightened daughter—just to hold her and tell her everything would be okay—and she shrieked as the blade went into her side with one quick, hot jab.

Shelley backed away, crying out at the sight of Virginia's blood on her hands. Virginia grabbed the knife and attempted to pull it out, coughing and moaning as the blade held deep inside her. The fur all along her arms and in the front of the coat became red and matted.

Virginia looked at Shelley, shocked and brokenhearted. "My baby!" she whispered, her face cold with tears, as she dizzily stumbled to her knees.

"Virginia!" George called from just around a bend.

Shelley continued to back away.

"Shelley!" Virginia cried. "Please don't leave me here!"

Shelley turned and ran, and then she disappeared from the trail into the overgrowth.

George spotted Virginia and rushed over to her. "Virginia?"

Virginia allowed George to take her into his arms, crying softly as she fought to remain conscious. He looked at the knife, afraid to touch it, gagging at the sight of so much blood. He held her head to his chest, closing his eyes for a moment, kissing her soft, sweet hair.

"I'm so sorry!" she cried, brushing her hand against his cheek.

"You have nothing to be sorry for," he said, trying to sound as calm as possible. He lifted her up and began to carry her down the path. "Just hold on! I'll find some help!"

"It was Shelley!" Virginia wailed. "Is Kurt here too?"

"The kids are safe at home," George said.

Virginia shook her head.

George did his best to quiet her. "Stay still—it's going to be okay! Everything's going to be okay!" A small crowd amassed as he staggered to the pavilion. He fell to his knees, cradling her in his shaking arms. "I need a doctor! Someone!"

Virginia stared up at him, tears streaming down her cheeks. "I can't believe you came," she said, and then her eyes rolled back, her eyelids fluttering and her body seizing for a moment. A slow breath escaped her, and then she fell limp and still. The sheen in her eyes went dull and lifeless, and George held her close, shamelessly crying aloud.

He burned Virginia's body before he left, but first he knotted up a lock of her silky hair and cut it off. He brought the lock up to his nose and smelled it, closing his eyes, and then he gently slid it into his shirt pocket. He covered Virginia's body with piles of dried grass, taking the better part of the night to clear a large enough area, find enough dry material, and arrange it all just so. He finished as the late night slowly moved toward early morning, and then he left her, promising that he would be back soon to finish the job.

He tried not to think too much as he worked through the bitter task, a strange numbness having taken over shortly after he had begun. Every once in a while, the pain would creep its way back and George would have to take a moment to compose himself, but he knew what he had to do. This was the one last gift he could give his wife: cremation, so her soul might rest with human dignity. Only deviants buried their dead, and only rats rotted out in the fields; Virginia was far better than either.

George backtracked to the market and then crossed to a path leading east. The entire shantytown was asleep, but cinders still glowed within the large fire pits. George found a long, clean piece of wood in a small woodpile, and then held it in the cinders of a nearby fire pit long enough to catch the far end. He hurried back, the raging flame nothing more than a smoldering ember by the time he finally returned to the body. He kissed her on the forehead.

"Goodbye, my love."

Cursing the world, he stepped back and touched the embers against the dry grass. It caught quickly, and George backed even further as the entire mound went up in flames.

He watched the giant fire for a short time then forced himself to begin the long walk back home. He had already gained some distance from the site when a small gust of wind threw part of the fire into the open field. The fire exploded across the broad area, burping up great masses of steam and black smoke as the remaining clusters of snow melted and made worthy attempts at stifling the blaze. The fire continued to grow, however, the wind slowly moving it toward the deviant market and the adjacent shantytowns.

George continued, oblivious as the wind picked up and beat against his weary body. He persisted, pushing through the slushy, muddy remnants of the snow, ignoring his misery, praying that he might somehow find a way to preserve both his job and his family's home.

All he had left were Kurt and Shelley. If it hadn't been for the two of them, he would have simply stayed by Virginia's side until the elements carried him to her and the pain became no more. He knew, however, that his children needed him, and he kept the image of their faces in his mind to give himself the strength to keep going.

# Chapter Thirty-One

Shelley wandered through the empty field, turning to spot the fire in the distance as the smell of smoke hit her. She prayed silently that the fire would wipe out every last deviant in the district.

Disturbing images tore through her mind, and the bloodstains across her jacket paid as a reminder of her horrifying encounter. She knew there was no way that thing she had stabbed could have been her mother, and yet it had sounded so much like her and behaved as if it really had *thought* it was her. It had seemed almost . . . distraught over Shelley's refusal to buy into its ruse. The image of the deviant with its hands in the air, the blue glitter slipping from its fingers, flashed in her mind, and Shelley reaffirmed in her mind that she had done the right thing by stabbing it.

Still, she couldn't push the images from her mind. Her emotions ran high, as if she were reliving the event repeatedly in one endless, hellish loop. Kurt's cold face made an unexpected visit among the other images, sending her into heavy fits of despair. She continued on, however, eating small patches of remaining snow to keep from dehydrating and reciting her favorite poetry as loudly as she could in an attempt to drown out all of her other thoughts.

She slowed when she reached a narrow trail carved between the field and a sea of makeshift houses. The shantytown consisted mostly of small plywood buildings that connected like cubicles in a giant workroom. There were fire pits situated strategically between the structures, each placed just far enough from the cheap, rotting shacks to keep them from catching and turning the entire town into one giant bonfire. Large boiling pots and skewered rats sizzled over the flames beside jars of stagnant water and stacks of rotten firewood.

Shelley quietly moved across the outskirts of the squalid town, observing the dirty, ignorant-eyed people as she passed them. They took turns staring over at her, whispering about her among one another as they huddled together and carefully watched to make sure she was not accompanied by a gang. Their eyes told her that she was unwelcome there, but she kept her distance and no one moved to run her off.

She kept a straight face, biding her time, holding her hungry stomach. She wondered what thoughts might be going through their simple, little minds—and whether they could guess the hateful, vindictive thoughts that ran through hers. The longer she stared at them, the more the deviants looked like the vermin that ran through their dirt paths and roasted over their fires. Walking along the edge of the shantytown, seeing these people in their element, Shelley could finally see them for what they were: senseless, feral animals that did nothing but create a wake of filth and disease wherever they went.

She scowled when a few of the deviants had the audacity to laugh at her, whispering amongst themselves and staring her down. What did they have to laugh about? Were they proud to be such lowly creatures? Didn't they know how much better she was than them? She couldn't help but laugh back, picturing them as the filthy, giant rats they were, chattering off about nothing but their own stupidity.

She kept to the far edge of the path, holding her bag ready in case any of them decided to become hostile, laughing and pointing back as she passed the group. Had their numbers been fewer, she would have crushed in each of their skulls without hesitation, but she knew there were too many for her to take them on all at once. She glanced behind her one last time before disappearing down a path cutting through a field of overgrowth.

No one followed her. If they had, she'd have killed them. That was her purpose now.

Exterminating rats.

She glanced up at the sky, falling into a daze of grief and uncertainty. What appeared to be cloud cover obscured her view of the stars, but she watched them anyway.

"What a day," she breathed, then stopped and turned at the smell of smoke.

Her heart sped up as she realized the entire field to one side of her was on fire. She heard screams in the distance.

From where she stood, the giant flame looked like the head of a demon, ravenously swallowing up all in its path, and Shelley knew that everything in the vicinity would soon be black and dead. She ran as fast as she could through the tall grass, the fire quickly spreading behind her. She heard continuing screams and intermittent hisses as the deviants tried to douse the inferno with their last rations of water. The thought of it made her giddy.

She felt a hot gust, then the heavy rush of smoke as she raced the flames to a nearby hill. Excitement turned to panic when she realized the flames were suddenly upon her. Her eyes stung and she choked as the air all around her grew thick with smoke. She dropped her backpack, unwilling to carry the weight any longer, but still the fire gained on her. Just a little louder . . . just a little darker . . . just a little hotter every second . . . until finally there was nowhere left to run and the searing black hell engulfed her screaming, writhing body.

# Chapter Thirty-Two

It took George the better part of two days to find his way home. He persisted, forcing himself to keep moving despite the intense malady and fever the HD-1 virus caused him. He felt as though he might collapse at any time from the drain of the long walk combined with his rising fever. By the time George got to the main shuttle garages, he was too distracted to notice that the halls were unusually empty and only a few of the shuttles were running. He passed only a handful of people, including a lone security associate on the way from the garage to his building. All was quiet when he began up the stairs that led to his floor.

He slowly moved down the hall, his body stiff and sore from the exhausting journey. He slowed as he reached his apartment. Relieved that his key still fit, he opened the door. The apartment was cold and dark, and he entered apprehensively. He closed the door behind him and turned on the kitchen light.

He stumbled back as he saw the writing on the kitchen wall, gasping at the hateful black words smudged across the flat whitewash. At first, he thought his apartment had fallen victim to some random vandal. When he saw Shelley's signature at the bottom, near the floor, his body shuddered and his heart sank.

"Shelley? Kurt?" he called out.

He searched the apartment. There were dirty dishes in the sink, crusted with old tomato sauce and dried spaghetti. Kurt's school bag was missing and Shelley's room looked like it had been searched, but there were no other clues to help him determine what had happened or how long the apartment had been vacant. Perhaps Family-Corp had stepped in after he had been missing for a day or two and Shelley and Kurt were back at Safe House, waiting for him to return.

George turned on the wall heater and sat down for a moment, ready to pass out. He sweated profusely, although a cold chill ran endlessly up and down his achy back. The room began to spin, forcing him to close his eyes. He got to his feet and made his way to the sink. The water was cold, and it felt good against his face. He cupped a small amount in his hands and swallowed one sweet, refreshing sip, knowing his sour stomach would not likely accept much more.

He went back to the heater and sat down, his body shivering, although fatigue called him to his bed. He took off his jacket, tossing it to the back of another chair, his heart skipping for a moment when he noticed just how much blood had soaked into the thick material. The warmth against his back did nothing to ease the wet chill that moved through his body. He decided to go to the bedroom to put on a dry change of clothes and lie down for a while.

He froze as he entered the room, spotting the box that had been told held Virginia's remains, and suddenly the sight of the phony keepsake sent him fuming. He grabbed the box and hurled it across the room, and ash erupted out of it in a thick cloud as it hit the wall and broke open.

George rifled through his clean clothes and then slowly peeled away the layers he had worn for the past several days. As he hit the last layer, he realized he was in desperate need of a shower, and he grabbed his clean clothes and hurried into the bathroom.

He turned on the click-light and started the shower, then he turned to look at his shaggy face in the mirror. Much to his surprise, his eye color was in the process of changing. The very center of his iris was still brown, but the rest of it had become ice blue. He stared at the terrifying marvel for a moment, then forced himself to turn away. He showered and dressed as if nothing were wrong, then went to bed with Virginia's pillow in his arms and waited for the fever to render him senseless.

GEORGE WOKE with a start, shivering in the darkness, realizing that the wall heater had gone cold. He looked around the apartment, feeling disoriented in the unbroken darkness. He felt his way to the front door and slowly opened it. To his surprise, the hallway was also dark.

He made his way to the shuttle hall, and then stood motionless as he opened the door and peered out. The fluorescent lights overhead buzzed and flickered, seemingly struggling to stay on. All else was silent and still. A light stench permeated the air. George struggled to remain standing as he surveyed the bodies.

His eyes went wide, panic taking hold. "Hello? Anyone?" he called as loudly as his dry, sore throat would allow.

He passed over the body of a young woman who stared wide-eyed into oblivion. She had pale deviant eyes, and yet she wore an Education-Corp uniform. George moved away from the body. He passed another open-eyed corpse, noticing that it too posed a mixture of deviant eyes and higher-class attire. He began to scan all of the nearby bodies, finding all of them to be deviants.

He glanced up at the central air unit, noticing that intermittent gusts of glittery powder trickled from them, slowly settling to the ground. He looked down, realizing that the ground was covered with a combination of blue and green dust.

"Hello?" he yelled.

No reply.

He hurried back to his apartment and made his way to the bathroom. He turned on the click-light, his weary body shaking and sweating. A terrified whimper escaped his lips as he huddled in the corner of the small room, beneath the imagined safety of the dim, battery-powered light. He closed his eyes, hoping he might open them back up to find that this was all some twisted nightmare, that he might awaken, refreshed and renewed, to the realization that the world as he knew it would continue.

His eyes snapped back open, but to his horror, the grim reality remained.

# ABOUT THE AUTHOR

Leigh M. Lane has been writing mixed-genre science fiction and horror for over twenty years. She currently resides in the dusty outskirts of Sin City with her husband, Thomas, an editor and educator who shares her passion for literature.

Among her other works are dystopian thriller and *World-Mart* prequel, *The Private Sector*, Gothic horror *Finding Poe*, dark science fantasy *Myths of Gods*, and dystopian cyberpunk *The Corruption*.

For more about Leigh M. Lane and her other works, visit her website at http://www.cerebralwriter.com.

Printed in Great Britain
by Amazon

20371533R00169